Part Fourteen

FOXHOLE

"*The man of thought who will not act is ineffective; the man of action who will not think is dangerous.*"

\- Richard M. Nixon

VINCE

Vince was in the lead truck when they left French Lick on Highway 56, then onto Highway 150.

In normal times, they could have spent most of the route on Highway 150, which would have taken them through some medium-sized towns. The plan was to avoid population centers until they got closer to Chicago and dodge medium-sized cities if it could be done and large cities like Indianapolis at all costs. It was best to stay off the expressways while still moving as fast as they could. It was important to not move so fast they didn't have enough time to react to obstacles in the road. They couldn't be sure obstacles were left in the road by accident or on purpose, and either could be deadly with too much speed. While this early in the crisis Vince didn't think the criminals and looters would have banded together yet in gangs with a plan like creating roadblocks to attack travelers, it was better to be safe and plan as if there was than expect they weren't and be sorry.

An old SEAL Vince worked with in Afghanistan always said, "*Slow is smooth and smooth is fast.*" Vince kept thinking of that during this trip.

On the route up Highway 150 west from French Lick, the men were on alert for obvious chokepoints. All three had experience in the Middle East with the deadly results of roadside attacks. They were on guard for locations where people might try to attack or slow them down. The first obstacle Vince worried about was a bridge over the East Fork White River at Shoals, Indiana. When they approached the bridge, Vince radioed Andy and Dwight in the second vehicle to hang back in an overwatch position while Vince moved across. As soon as he made it through and determined it was safe, he radioed for them to follow him across. Since this was a very rural location, Vince didn't think the odds of encountering an issue here was very high. However, with the way things were going and the importance of this mission, it was best to be in a high state of vigilance at all times.

After Shoals, the next town they passed through was Loogotee, not much more than a sign on the road and a few buildings. Vince kept the two vehicles moving fast with about forty yards between them. Later in the journey, they would have to find safe spots to rest. For now, the plan was to watch for traps and chokepoints and make good time while they were in the rural areas. After Loogotee, they would take Highway 231 north through Farlen and then Bloomfield, working their way through central Indiana. Eventually the dense population areas would be harder to avoid. When that happened, they would head northeast into Chicago via a series of surface streets and neighborhoods. That was when the risk and danger would be at its highest.

Even this early in the trip, the feeling was surreal. Occasionally they would pass a small town or farm where people were working and going about their business as usual. Other times they would pass people walking or biking as if time had rolled back fifty years. In areas with more businesses or denser population, they would see a burned building, car wreck, or signs of a gunfight that reminded them of a war zone. During one of the radio checks between him and Andy, Vince made the remark that the goal was not to be the source of those gunfights but to always get through before or after they happened. Having to say that grated on Vince because he was a protector by nature and wanted to help. In this case, his mission was clear. The people he needed to help were on a block in Chicago, and they needed him.

Not all the people walking or watching them pass were victims. Some were predators. Vince knew those types would be more of a threat when they banded together and made a better plan with their roadblocks or their attacks on other survivors.

The first time they prepared to pass under an expressway, Vince stopped them a ways back. They hiked up the embankment to assess the expressway both east and west. They could see wrecks on the road and a shantytown in the distance where it appeared as if people looted the crashed semis and then just set up camp. In an odd way, it made sense because that was where the food was and the route many people would take. They climbed back down the bank and resumed their journey, confident in the choice to avoid the expressways.

Vince was now sure he was making this trip in the nick of time. While it was possible the government would get things back together, it didn't make sense to wait and hope. He definitely didn't want to gamble with his girls' lives that way.

He dreaded the thought of going through Gary, Indiana, resolving to stick to his plan and go around the large population centers even if it cost more time. As bad as he thought Indianapolis could be, he imagined Gary would be like a war zone, because it hadn't been much better before. It bothered Vince that they were driving so much slower than he wanted. Even though his head told him they were doing this right, his heart hated that they stopped so often to make sure the way was safe. He reconciled himself to the fact that if he didn't do this right, he might leave his girls stranded in Chicago. It was only the strength of his training that kept him to the plan.

One of their checkpoints along the route was a Wal-Mart Supercenter on Highway 231, where they wanted to turn north onto Highway 54. There was a large police presence and a lot of people with trucks and tables set up there. It appeared to be a farmer's market and flea market rolled into one, complete with police protection. If Wal-Mart was helping and the police were making sure things were kept orderly, it could be a good thing. In either event, Vince and the team kept moving.

Soon, they turned on to a narrow county road heading north to take them to Highway 48. Although it was a very circuitous route, Vince was convinced it was the safest way. They stayed on 48 as it turned into Highway 59 to avoid Terre Haute. Terre Haute wasn't a huge city, but it was approaching the size Vince thought could be a risk. On Highway 59, they passed through the towns of Clay City, Ashboro, and Brazil with the same tactics and level of care they used earlier in the day. As they headed north then turned west on Highway 231 and north again on Highway 41, Vince noticed more destruction and therefore danger. He didn't know if the damage was worse and there truly were more predators this far north or if it was only his growing apprehension putting him on edge. While Vince was frustrated this was taking all day, he had to admit that they were making good time, all things considered.

Highway 41 took them through Turkey Run State Park. It was getting late and darker. Vince wanted to consult his map and get some food in his stomach. All three of them were hungry and needed a break. It was important that they be rested and nourished when they hit the most dangerous spots. Vince found an old barn off the side of the road near the state park that was on its last legs yet could still fit both vehicles inside. While the men were new to each other, they were experienced campaigners and easily fell into the routine of camp the same way they had when driving the trucks in convoy formation. While one of the men put together a meal of both MREs and ramen noodles to fill them up and add some carbs, another took first watch, observing the perimeter through loose boards in the barn. Walking outside would have provided a better range of vision but would have made them easier to spot by others. They decided a view from inside would be good enough.

Vince studied the map. He verified the route he'd planned back at Gus's place. He assumed they would be fairly safe up to Peotone, Illinois. After Peotone when they were on Highway 50 or the Governor's Highway, things would get dicier.

That was tomorrow. Tonight, they needed rest. Vince tried the SAT phone again and couldn't get through. That was frustrating and was sure to make his sleep more restless until it was his time to stand guard. Vince ate and then found a dark corner of the barn to sack out because he had the middle watch.

DAVE

Dave was receiving reports from the different locations.

The most urgent calls were from people who had been on the fence about joining the communities before. Many of them formerly balked at the personal service commitment. Some disliked the insistence that people with critical skill sets would be given a subsidy, making them equals. Those people were now eager to agree that the plan was fantastic. Dave snorted when contemplating the wealthy business leaders, corporate lawyers, and surgeons who had previously detested sharing equality and living space with mechanics and farmers who now thought it was a great idea.

Many new investors were rushing to join the charter towns in various stages of development in their area. The longer the civil unrest lasted and the more cities it encompassed, the more panicked people became. While some were contacting Dave's company through proper channels, more were just walking up to the construction sites or gates, checkbook in hand, trying to join. Most were being turned away. While Dave welcomed an increased understanding of the value of this project, he didn't want to relax the admission standards. The standard investor would have to wait and follow the regular path to membership. For now, if someone had a needed skill and passed an interview and background check, they would be welcomed as long as there was space.

In the long run, having a higher mix of people with critical skill sets was not as profitable as the cross-section of people he originally planned for. Yet if this crisis didn't end, traditional monetary profits wouldn't matter. If it did end, there would be time to invite those who had the means but not all of the skills. Others with less essential skills or who only had money would have to wait until the nation recovered.

The other groups of people who were calling Dave's office were construction supervisors and project managers. They wanted to know if they should keep working and what to do about workers who didn't show up for work. They wanted to make sure they would be paid and how. Dave pushed them all to keep going full steam ahead. He promised payment, and if the dollar was devalued they could be paid in goods or gold. Dave was prepared. Not surprisingly, many of the workers wanted to trade their services for a safe place to live with their families. Dave made sure that Louis issued instructions that those workers would get priority in the screening and background check process. While there wasn't room for everyone, they could take on some of the best and most qualified. This was the time to get the communities done and offer bonuses to those workers who did show up. For the people who had already moved in, it was time to take up arms and protect their homes and communities.

Dave received an update from Vince and Ellie. Vince was still south of Chicago, and Ellie spoke with Liz. They were all trying to connect up, and the fact that they hadn't yet concerned him more than he wanted to admit. He would be on pins and needles until he got word Liz and her people made it safely to Ellie's place.

LIZ

The group was exhausted from the trek through Chicago. They rested in the old auto repair building while waiting for Malcolm. They could still hear occasional screams or the explosion of gunfire outside.

What was even more chilling was the occasional hysterical or drunken cackle of a pillager somewhere near. It was as if the worst elements of society were running loose and now ruled. Dusk was coming, and the plunderers would be on the hunt even more ravenously than they were during the day.

Soon they heard an engine revving down the alley behind the building and the sounds of garbage cans and debris being struck. Junior was closest to the door and peeked through a crack. A red minivan screeched to a stop, and the sliding side door opened. Malcolm jumped out as they were coming out of the back door of the building and told them to load up in a hurry. They piled into the van in a rush. As they were racing away, they could see a crowd coming down the alleyway behind them. Some in the crowd appeared desperate, others curious and hungry. Still more were angry and aggressive. Liz only knew they needed to be away from here.

Malcolm came to a main street. "It's only another block to where we need to go." As he was speaking, a group of men wearing red bandanas noticed the van and moved toward them. Many of them were armed. Malcolm yelled, "Plan B!" cut the wheel, and drove in another direction as fast as the van would go.

They paused momentarily in an alley, where Malcolm picked up a walkie talkie. "You there? It's me."

"Go ahead," replied a female voice.

"I need to come in hot on the south side. Let our people know the gang is a block away from the north blockade. They may follow me to the south end of the block or come at the north end. Just be ready."

"Gotcha. You're coming in hot from the south. The bad guys are stirred up."

Malcolm floored the accelerator, still holding the press-to-talk button with his right hand on the walkie talkie. "I saw Raheem and Malik with the gang, so they know where I'm going. What they don't know is which end of the block I'm coming in through, so this all has to happen fast."

"Those guys don't give up," the female voice responded in weary exasperation. *"This is getting old, but we'll be ready."*

Malcolm dropped the walkie talkie into the center console and gunned the engine, making hard and fast turns. He scraped paint alongside of a wall to avoid running down a few sketchy-looking vagrants. Although Malcolm had a kind heart and didn't want to hurt anyone, he was running full blast and wanted to get everyone home safe. Scraping the wall endangered them because they could have disabled the van. He drove straight at two cars parked sideways blocking the entrance to the block on North Kilpatrick Avenue, where he and Ellie lived. Scarcely fifty yards before hitting the blockade, a car was rolled out of the way, and he rushed through.

There were only a couple of dozen people still living on the block. A few had been injured or killed. Some had never come home from work or wherever they'd been when things went from bad to worse. Even more chose to leave and try to make it to safety elsewhere.

They stopped in the narrow driveway beside Ellie and Vince's home, the relief among the group palpable. When they got out of the van, the remaining neighbors rushed to meet Liz and hear what she'd seen outside the block. Her heart was beating faster than if she'd just stepped off a huge rollercoaster. While she was a star in her own right as an actress, they were all stars right now because they'd been out there amid all the chaos, on foot, and survived.

After the talking and well-wishing was done, Ellie invited Liz and her group inside. She lived in a tastefully decorated two-story home. Ellie offered Liz, Carol, and Junior something to drink as well as a place to clean up. "The utilities and water work sometimes, and other times not. The water pressure is too low for a shower. However, enough trickles out for a bath if you can live with six or eight inches of water. To make it warm, Malcolm can heat some water on the barbecue grill to add to it."

Liz gratefully accepted for all of them since Carol was too shell-shocked to respond and Junior was too proud to ask for warm water to clean up.

Part Fifteen

STRATEGY AND TACTICS

"*Is there any instinct more deeply implanted in the heart of man than the pride of protection, a protection which is constantly exerted for a fragile and defenseless creature?*"

- Honoré de Balzac

VINCE

Vince was the last to roll out of the sack in the morning. It was about two a.m. He didn't want to admit that these schedules were getting harder on him as he got older. He never slept well during a mission anyway.

Mid-day to midnight was the time when the criminal element was most active. They hunted, partied, fornicated, fought, and killed most during those hours. If you wanted to avoid them, you hunkered down if you could when they were most active and made time when they were sleeping. That schedule wasn't foolproof and couldn't always be adhered to, but it was the best plan for now.

Vince spoke to Dwight to try and lighten the mood when discussing his plan for their schedule. "You know the old saying, 'If you try to invent a foolproof plan, someone will just build a better fool'?" Right now, the world was full of fools. The breakdown of society was weeding out the bad fools from the better fools by the thousands. Anything that tipped the scales in their favor before the better fools got their game together helped.

They planned to be on the road by 2:30 a.m. and get about twelve hours of movement under their belt before settling in for the night again. If all went perfectly, they would be at Ellie's tonight. If not, the hope was it went well enough that they would find a warehouse or abandoned building to hunker down in by that time outside of the densest part of Chicago proper. If that happened, he wanted to make sure they were left with the quickest route through the city for the final run to Ellie's.

Vince cursed himself for not driving the route months before everything erupted. As a soldier, and more importantly as a dad, he needed to be prepared. He should have had a good lay of the land. The fact that he hadn't wanted to intrude on Ellie, Kate, and Malcolm's new life and home was a lame excuse that rang hollow now that they were in need and his efforts were hampered by his lack of knowledge. As someone who believed in being prepared, he should have planned that "something" might happen. This was his ex-wife and daughter's new home, and he should know it well enough to have a good mental picture of the ins and outs of where they lived and how to get there. Ellie had only been there for a few months, and the wounds were still raw. He always thought there would be more time.

They were on Highway 41 headed through Veedersburg. Everything was going well so far. Much of the good luck was probably due to it being so early in the morning. The next town, Attica, concerned Vince because the bridge over the Wabash presented another natural chokepoint and a good place for an ambush. Even though they were making good time, Vince and the others couldn't relax. They were already experiencing more delays than yesterday. There were too many stalled vehicles for his comfort. Either things had been much worse here or the bad guys were much faster at organizing to make narrow traffic channels along the route for an attack. So far, either Vince's team appeared too formidable to take on or the bandits were sleeping off a drunk and would attack other travelers later in the day.

Highway 41 was technically a back road and a better choice than the expressway. It still was a main thoroughfare locally and a good option for predators. The plan was to get through fast. It was morning and the sun was up as they approached the town of Attica. They slowed when Vince recognized the roadblock out front comprised of old cars and sawhorses in front and police cruisers behind the blockade.

Vince keyed the walkie talkie. "Andy, you and Dwight fall back about seventy-five yards behind me and take an overwatch position." The plan wasn't to hide but to not present an easy target either. The thought was that Vince could find out what was going on with the roadblock while Andy and Dwight covered him from behind far enough away that they could provide fire support yet not so close they made an easy target for those at the roadblock if they had bad intentions. "One of you should dismount and work around a perimeter in the woods near the trucks, keep an eye out for traps or ambush sites."

While Vince still didn't know Andy and Dwight well, giving instructions came naturally to him. They didn't hesitate to follow his lead. When he got within twenty yards of the roadblock, Vince stopped the truck, slung his AR single-point harness over his neck, and pushed the gun behind him. Many times, a single point was for amateurs and show. Yet it did have its uses in a quick reaction, urban warfare situation with a shorter barreled weapon and optics that could take the banging around. The current configuration he was using had EOtech optics and a laser underneath. He would be in and out of the truck and moving fast, not sniping from a distance. Vince kept his hands clear of his sidearm and held them palm out as he walked to the barricade.

"That's far enough," a man said in a gravelly voice.

Vince stopped. "We only want to pass through."

"I'm the sheriff here," the man called back. "The town is closed."

The yelling across the distance was getting to Vince, and he asked, "Mind if I approach?"

"Only if you're unarmed," said the sheriff. "If I see so much as an ankle gun or pocket knife, I shoot to kill."

Vince held up a finger and walked back to the truck. He picked up the walkie and keyed the mike. "Andy, I'm going closer I'm going in unarmed at their request."

"I'd advise against that," Andy warned.

Vince had a good feeling about this sheriff, and he needed info. More than that, he needed to get through the town and across that bridge. "I understand," he said to Andy. "I'm going in, though. Don't let Dwight get close to town and mess this up."

Vince disarmed and left everything in the truck, including the walkie talkie. He walked back up to the barricade and stuck out his hand. "I'm Vince Cavanaugh."

The sheriff hesitated, gazed off in the distance, and spat chewing tobacco on the ground. "I'm Sheriff Tom Cooper." Finally, he shook Vince's hand. "We closed the town after some looters raped, killed, and stole from a few in town. We'd been allowing people through the city with only a couple of checkpoints at the few roads that come into and out of the city. We told people as they entered that they couldn't stay but were guaranteed safe passage through the city. One car didn't come out the other side, and no one noticed till later that night. When one of my deputies got home from working the roadblock, he found his wife and two daughters raped and murdered in his own home."

"Damn!" Vince exhaled from deep in his lungs.

"The hell of it was that the two scumbags were still there. Drunk as hell, listening to music from a radio plugged into the deputy's generator. He killed them on the spot and fed them to the hogs on a neighbor's farm. He then took his wife and girls to the cemetery and dug the graves himself. He was filling them back in when we found him and helped. He told us the story and kept working until he tamped down the last spade of dirt. Then he took out his service revolver and shot himself before I could stop him. I dug the last grave myself, and now no one goes through my city. No one."

It was clear the other deputies knew the story and were angry and wary of outsiders. Vince's heart ached for that deputy in the way only another dad could feel. He was speechless.

After a pause, Sheriff Cooper said, "We did get notice from the governor that the military and National Guard are working to restore order. That help could take months to reach a small town like this. When that day comes, I will hang up this gun and retire to a cabin I have in the forest and be done. Until that burden is taken from my shoulders, I'll do whatever I can to keep this town safe, and that means no one coming through."

When the sheriff finished speaking, he turned and walked off a bit to be by himself. One of the deputies nearby stepped closer to Vince and said in a low tone, "Don't push him. I shouldn't be telling you this, but that deputy he told you about was his son-in-law. Those girls were his daughter and granddaughters."

That story made Vince sick at his stomach and eager to get back on the road to his own daughter. He didn't know what to do and was unsure of next steps for the first time in this mission. "Is it true that the Army and National Guard are coming?" he asked, mostly to buy time to think.

"It's true inasmuch as they have good intentions," the deputy answered. "I was in the room when the message came across the shortwave. I know the military is stretched thin, and lots of Guardsmen are not reporting for duty. So many of them chose to stay home and protect their families and ignore the call up that it's hampering the Guards' ability to respond. Anyway, there's some backroads you can take to get around the city and head north again."

As the deputy described the route around the city, Vince worked hard to control his anger and frustration at the potentially deadly delay. This detour would cost them too much time and risk. It could mean the difference of life and death to his family. After thanking the deputy, Vince again approached the sheriff. While the sheriff was still staring off in the distance, Vince asked to speak. The sheriff nodded.

"Sir," Vince began, "I know you all have experienced some hardship in this town, and probably personally as well."

"My deputy talks too much," the sheriff muttered under his breath.

"I have a proposal to make, Sheriff. I only make this because I'm desperately trying to get my ex-wife and daughter and a few other women out of Chicago. As bad as things have been here, you can imagine how much worse they are in the city. As a family man, you must know how much this detour hurts my mission and my heart. These few hours could be the difference between life and death for them."

This earned Vince a moment of side-eye contact from the sheriff.

Emboldened, Vince continued. "I know how much a man's honor and word are worth. As much as I need you to break your word, I won't ask it."

That earned raised eyebrows from the sheriff.

"What I will say is this. You're still the sheriff, and you still wear the badge. My two friends and I are armed in your jurisdiction. I'm sure there is a penalty for that. I suggest some hard labor. If you were to cuff me to the back of that black truck I came in with and I had to push it the length of your fine city, would that about cover my debt?"

Sheriff Cooper paused and stared out over the fields for a couple of minutes, then walked away stone faced. Vince felt both rage and despair at his failure.

When he heard the sheriff say to his deputy, "Arrest that man," with a nod toward Vince, he wasn't sure if he should be elated or if this was a real arrest. The sheriff peered at Vince in a stern, angry way, maybe partially regretting his decision, and said gruffly, "Do you want to call your men in or do we have to go get 'em?"

"I'll call them," Vince said.

The deputy escorted Vince to his truck. In cuffed hands, he picked up the walkie talkie. "Andy, I need both you and Dwight down here on the double. Leave the weapons in the truck and no shenanigans."

When Vince set down the walkie talkie, the deputy asked, "Why didn't you tell them you were all three under arrest?"

"Because these are very experienced special operators, I need to look them in the eye and let them know we don't need rescuing, and the sheriff is only doing his job."

"I don't know what you and the sheriff have cooked up," the deputy said, his face grim. "I'll tell you this, though. That man has been through too much. If you let him down, I'll take you out like a dog, no questions asked. He's like a father to me and many of us on the force."

"I have no intention of letting him down." Vince matched the deputy's serious glare with one of his own. "I know I only met him for the first time a few minutes ago, yet I respect him and what he's doing. He's doing a hard job during hard times, and I admire that. I won't fight his directions."

When Andy and Dwight parked their truck alongside Vince's and got out unarmed, Vince said, "I need you both to remove any knives or hidden guns and drop them in the truck." They both paused and exchanged sideways glances. Vince stared them both in the eye and used his command voice from his military days to make his point, "Now!" Andy complied right away. Dwight still hesitated.

"Dwight," Vince said in a calmer tone, "I need your trust on this. I know you haven't been with me long. I won't let you down."

Dwight finally complied.

"Now for the hard part," Vince said. "We're all three under arrest for violating the town's conceal carry laws. Please trust me and let the deputy cuff you."

Vince was worried Dwight would bolt or fight back at this moment, but he accepted it easier than Andy did. With a bit of betrayal in their eyes, both men allowed themselves to be cuffed.

Then the sheriff walked up and said to the deputy, "I have no intention of feeding and housing these vagrants. I do, however, think the judge would agree that making them perform hard labor in front of the townspeople as an example would be an appropriate punishment for their crimes."

The deputy wore a funny expression and looked at the sheriff as if he'd lost his mind. "Sheriff, I don't know what we have in the way of hard labor. Do you want them to chop wood or something?"

"No," Sheriff Cooper said. "Cuff them to the back of their trucks and make them shove the trucks around town a bit until they're worn out, sweaty, and the townspeople have seen their punishment. You can let a couple of the young boys steer the trucks while these men push."

"Okay," the deputy said, drawing out the word. This was the strangest bit of police work he'd ever been a part of. "How much time should they push and what should I do with them when they are done?"

"They don't have to push much longer than it takes to get them all lathered up and appreciative of our laws," Sherriff Cooper responded. "When you're done, make sure they're out of our town. I don't care where. The bridge on the other side of the Wabash might be an option, though. That will teach them a lesson." The sheriff walked off.

By now, the deputy was grinning. "He must like you," he said to Vince. "I hope you don't mind a little work and some catcalls. This ought to be fun."

It didn't work out that way.

Vince smiled and teased and turned on a charm the men never suspected he had. Halfway through, the kids of the town were helping him push and the ones who weren't pushing Vince's truck rode in the bed of Andy and Dwight's truck, making it harder for them to push. Some people had a knack for making things work out for them.

Dwight thought Vince was a good man to follow and probably a bad man to fight. Very few people knew Dwight well. Those who did knew him as a reader and somewhat of a philosopher. Once he figured out what Vince had planned, he chortled to himself as he pushed and thought of a line from Sun Tzu and *The Art of War*: *"He will win who knows when to fight and when not to fight."*

When they got to the bridge, the sheriff was nowhere to be seen. Many of the townspeople were there cheering and laughing with the kids who had played along.

The deputy gave Vince a strong handshake. "This town needed something to smile about. Thanks, and I mean that sincerely. If I can do you a good turn sometime, just let me know."

DAVE

Dave wanted to call Vince.

Sitting and waiting for an update was driving him crazy. Still, Vince would be on the move, and he didn't need the distraction. He did call Ellie, whom he'd always had a soft spot for. It hurt Dave a lot when she and Vince divorced. It took several tries to get through on the SAT phone. When Ellie answered, she sounded frazzled. Dave was proud that she didn't let it stop her from what needed to be done. She reported they were doing well and that Liz and her team made it to her house, although they'd lost a member of their team along the way.

Ellie enjoyed talking to Dave. He had a way of making her feel comforted and at ease. He had that effect on a lot of people. Perhaps that was a part of why he'd been so successful in business. She told Dave that Liz was a pleasure to be around, not like some spoiled Hollywood star Ellie had worried she might be. Kate was on cloud nine getting to talk to Liz. Kate peppered Liz with questions about Hollywood and different stars. Eventually Ellie had to pull Kate away so Liz could get some sleep.

Dave asked to talk to Kate, mostly because he was missing his family. It could be lonely in his mountain retreat. Talking to Kate always made him smile. He could get so caught up in her world and her infectious personality and energy. They talked about his new home in the mountains, her school, and her impressions of Liz. Finally, Dave hung up and got back to the business at hand. He'd begun to worry that the charter towns were too exposed and well known. It needed to be done in the past to attract investors. Now was the time to make people forget about them. He made a mental note to follow up with his leadership team on how to best hide these locations in plain sight so they would blend into the white noise of the public psyche.

LIZ

Liz woke to sunlight streaming through the slits in the blinds and hitting her face. She could see the dust motes dancing in the sunbeams. She hadn't slept this deeply in days. The sheets were clean, the bed comfortable, and she could smell coffee brewing. The sounds and smells were the normal waking sounds of a regular home on a normal day. It was so incongruous after the last few days.

Liz pivoted on the bed to put her feet on the floor and rubbed the sleep from her eyes. She noticed clean clothes and house slippers waiting for her on the chair beside the bed. That made her smile and brought a tear to her eyes. There was some sanity and goodness left in the world. Although getting here had been incredibly hard, being here was the right move.

There was an old fashioned washbasin in her room. It had probably been an antique *objet d'art* a few weeks ago. Now it was ready for use again with a matching pitcher filled with steaming water next to it and a towel and washcloth draped over the back. Whoever tiptoed in to fill it and leave the clothes was probably what woke her up. She washed her face and body the best she could from the basin, much like people would have done a hundred and fifty years ago. She brushed her teeth with a toothbrush left at the basin, still packaged new from the store. When she dressed to go downstairs, she felt refreshed.

Liz was the last one in the room. She didn't feel guilty as she might have had she been this late to her grandmother's kitchen. The others were conversing in low tones to avoid waking her. She was shocked to see a casual breakfast going on and people in good spirits, eating. She was astounded to see eggs, sausage, and toast cooked on a griddle laid over top of the barbecue coals on the screened-in porch.

The conversation paused when she appeared. Ellie saw the surprise on her face at seeing the spread and chuckled. "It's the last of the perishable food Malcolm stocked up on. Gas for the generator is running low, and we know we will need to leave soon, so we might as well enjoy."

Before the conversation got serious again, Kate broke in anxiously. "Can I ask you something?"

Liz smiled, knowing her own nieces and nephews were just as interested about the Hollywood scoop when she visited the family farm. Kate surprised her by not asking more about Hollywood. Instead, she wanted to know more about Liz's childhood and the family farm in Kentucky.

"I'm from Kentucky too, and my dad and grandmother still live there," Kate said in a rush. "My grandmother has a farm near the Ohio River east of Louisville."

"My family's farm is in Trimble and Henry County!" Liz exclaimed. "They must be practically neighbors."

"How did you come to know Dave Cavanaugh?" Ellie asked.

Liz explained the details about the business venture and her manager's recommendation that she meet Dave. She admitted her own interest in who he was as a man on a more personal level.

Kate appeared confused. "Why do you want to be part of a charter town in Colorado if your family is in Kentucky?"

"Frankly, I never believed for real anything like this would be needed long term. I expected when there were riots or social unrest I would take a vacation to the mountains with other people in my social circle. Then a few weeks later we would just go back home. I never envisioned things going this bad for this long for real. If I thought I needed a place for months or years and had known Kentucky was an option, I'm pretty sure I would have chosen that location."

Malcolm cleared his throat. "We need to have a more serious talk. I want everyone in the house to be a part of the conversation." They moved to the living room, everyone finding a comfortable place to sit or stand. "I want to get straight to the point. Mr. Lewis was killed at the roadblock last night by some of the local gang members before we could run them off. I suppose it's a good thing his kids are married and living down south and that his wife passed from cancer last year. Even one death, though, diminishes us all, both spiritually and in defense of this block."

As Liz listened, she couldn't help but relive Frank's death on the way here.

"More concerning at the moment is the Jordan family," Malcolm said. "There were five of them with Thomas and Lena, their two sons, and teenage daughter. They disappeared during the night. There was no sign of bloodshed or violence at their home. I hope they made a run for a safer area and have not been kidnapped or worse."

"Didn't they have family in another part of the city?" Ellie asked.

"I think so," Malcolm responded, staring down at the paper towel he was twisting into knots. "I hope I'm not pushing people so hard to stay that they're afraid to tell me this isn't what they want. We're all more exposed when they leave and even more so when we aren't prepared."

That left them with only a handful of adults on the block, counting himself. Some of the others were getting nervous and talking about making a run for it. There was a block meeting scheduled later to discuss options.

"If the others choose to run, we will need to get out too. We can't hold out here on our own. The gang led by Raheem and his brother have an eye on this place. Still, I'm not sure where to go that's safe."

"My dad is coming to get us," Kate spoke up with a fierce note of pride.

Malcolm got along well with Kate and was coming to love her. This note of pride and confidence in her father tugged at his heart. He wanted to be the one that Ellie and Kate looked to with that confidence and enthusiasm. He wasn't the type to be insecure about his relationship with Ellie and her ex-husband. Seeing Vince through this lens as Kate did was different.

Part Sixteen

SO FAR

"It had long since come to my attention that people of accomplishment rarely sat back and let things happen to them. They went out and happened to things."

- Leonardo da Vinci

The meeting the previous night lasted for more than two hours and hadn't gone well. People were scared and wanted to run. Malcolm argued that if they ran, they'd be picked off one by one. They needed to either fort up and protect the block or retreat together. They did finally agree to stay another day and discuss it again. Most of the people who remained did so with the fading hope that the government would roll in and save them. Ellie wasn't sure how soon or even if that would happen. In either event, she didn't want to depend on it. She chuckled, thinking how much Vince had rubbed off on her over the years.

That afternoon Malcolm made sure they each had a backpack ready with essentials like water, food, and a change of clothes. He checked to ensure each person packed extra socks and a tarp or blanket in case they were forced to hike, and ensured the few guns they had were always close at hand and any spare ammo was packed and ready.

Malcolm and Ellie worked together to pack all their extra food, water, and ammo into plastics bins. They put the bins by the back door where the red minivan and a Ford Expedition were parked in the yard, close to the house. The idea was to be ready to leave at a moment's notice when they needed. Even so,

Malcolm didn't want to pack the cars yet in case they were stolen or fire bombed during the night.

That night, as Jeremiah Walker went to the south side barricade for his duty, he noticed it was unguarded and ran to get Malcolm. It was John Keselowski's turn to be on guard, and he was nowhere to be found. Steve Williams was supposed to be his backup, and he was gone too. Malcolm asked his older neighbor Mr. Goldberg to watch the barricade while he and Jeremiah went to search the neighborhood.

Mr. Goldberg, an older Jewish man whose family survived the German concentration camps, had asked to join Ellie's group on their trip south with Vince. All his friends were dead or gone, and he didn't think the city would get much better for a long time. He wanted to see what was in Kentucky. He didn't want to die in such a meaningless way as this would be if he stayed in his home and starved to death or was beaten to death by thugs for a few morsels of food or silver coins.

An inspection of the Keselowski home revealed that they had packed up and left in a hurry. Then they found Steve Williams asleep in his home. He had no idea what happened or why Malcolm was upset. He said that soon after he came to the blockade for his shift, John's wife came out and said she couldn't sleep and wanted some time with her husband. The two of them agreed to take the watch and told Steve to go home and get some sleep. At the time, he didn't think anything of it. Steve was genuinely surprised when Malcolm told him John and his wife were gone and the barricade was unguarded.

Malcolm's first move was to search the block and homes. He was most concerned that some of the gangsters could be hiding in one of the houses inside the barricades. They could be waiting for the opportunity to strike from behind. Although he didn't find any hidden intruders, what he did find was worse. Another family left along with the Keselowskis during the night, apparently wanting to get out without being asked questions or facing their neighbors. Malcolm wished they had at least been honest and not left the rest of them unguarded. Perhaps he was too vehement in last night's block meeting. His passion may have made them afraid to have a dissenting opinion.

In any event, the damage was done, and they didn't have the numbers to protect the block from a concerted effort by Raheem and his gang now. The best they could do was to keep up a show of strength until Vince got here.

When Malcolm took someone else out to the blockade to relieve Mr. Goldberg, he told him about the neighbors who left. Malcolm expected his elderly neighbor to be angry or scared. He was neither. He merely shared a quote from John Adams and trudged home. *"We live...in an age of trial. What will be the consequences, I know not."*

Malcolm moved the Walkers into his home. People were scared. The expressions on their faces struck him as a cross between the haunted look of people after a bombing and the frantic bearing of animals when a wildfire was headed their way.

———

By morning, the group was weary. It was more of a mental weariness of being on guard so long and hearing the gang's taunts and tests of the barricade for hours now. They'd heard the gang drinking and breaking things as they searched some homes outside their block. Those homes were on the other side of their barricade that was now more symbolic than useful. Malcolm believed the gang had gotten inside a few of the vacant homes inside the barricade through back doors or windows. Surprisingly, they hadn't tried to do more last night or this morning.

Ellie was too worried to make breakfast. Malcolm took her aside, hugged her, tried to lighten her spirits. "People need to see you be strong. You have to show confidence or the others will lose their nerve. It's not much longer. Vince should be here later today. Anyway, I'm hungry, and we can't take this food with us."

"Shouldn't we be packing or on guard? I'm so worried I don't know if I can be strong."

Malcolm smiled broadly. "I never did see a no good criminal wake up before noon. We need to get fed and full of pep, vim, and vigor before they come. Don't be moping around and bringing people down, most of all yourself. This is going to work out." He took her in his arms, and she hugged him back.

VINCE

After leaving the town of Attica and the Wabash River behind them, Vince and the men continued on Highway 41 toward Carbondale. Later they would pass through the towns of Boswell and Kentland. From there they would head west on 197th Street and then north on State Line Road.

They'd lost a great deal of time in Attica. Most of the travel since then was relatively uneventful, although they did encounter stalled cars and could see areas where there had obviously been violence. In contrast, they passed areas that appeared without problems. It reminded him of seeing a town after a tornado, where you could see two houses side by side and one was totally destroyed while the other was left untouched.

They turned onto West County Line Road for a short time, then north again on Highway 70. That would take them into Peotone, Illinois. He was anxious to get into Chicago. Interstate 57 went in roughly the same direction they wanted to go. If it was clear, it would be much faster. Even with his need to hurry and the temptation of the interstate, going the back roads through Peotone would avoid more conflict. Avoiding conflict meant a faster trip.

After Peotone, everything would get more densely populated as they got into Chicago proper. Denser population meant more risk. The plan was to avoid the densely populated areas when possible, and they needed to stick to it. When those areas couldn't be avoided, the plan was to go through them in the wee hours. Going through a town the size of Peotone in the late afternoon and then directly into Chicago didn't fit that plan. Vince fought to curb his impatience.

When they got closer to Peotone, Vince suggested they get the trucks off the road into a field behind some trees. They broke out some food and water and hastily ate a cold meal. During the break, Vince shared his thoughts with Andy and Dwight, who agreed it was better to be cautious and get there than be hasty and not get there at all. Peotone was large enough to create a risk to a crossing straight through and appeared dangerous. Vince checked the map for a way around the city.

Dwight offered up another option. "Boss, why don't I mosey on down to town and see what we have there?"

"I have to admit I'd like to have that intel. I can't take the chance of them spotting you, though, and being ready for us in the morning."

"They won't see me." Dwight had the dead, cold eyes of a killer that made Vince wonder once again what was in his past that he was hiding. It wasn't that he didn't trust Dwight; it was that the man kept secrets he wasn't ready to share yet.

As soon as he finished eating, Dwight spoke up. "It'll be dark soon. I'll be back in a bit."

Vince nodded as Dwight silently melted into the forest.

"Man, he creeps me out how he does that," Andy said. "I'm watching and I know he's leaving, and then it's like I miss it and he's gone."

"Some guys are just that good. I know a few, but they're few and far between."

"Yeah, well, I'll get some rest. Wake me if you want me to pull watch or something." He lay down and in the way of soldiers throughout time was instantly asleep in the shade of some bushes near the trucks.

Vince walked a watch patrol to allow his mind to sift through some of the events of the day and ponder what they might encounter tomorrow.

A couple of hours later, Dwight reappeared. It irked Vince that he didn't see him coming.

"We ought to get through Peotone now," Dwight said.

That got Vince's attention. "Why do you think so?"

"That town is buttoned up tight. I mean real tight. It reminds me of what a medieval town might have been like during a siege. You can tell there are areas where anything not barricaded and protected has already been looted or burned out. It feels like most of the criminal element has gone on to find easier pickings, but I can't be sure."

Vince thought about what Dwight shared. Out of the corner of his eye, he saw Andy rising to join them.

"The way things look to me, the townspeople will be out and about in the morning. If their defensive preparations are any indication, they won't welcome strangers," Dwight said.

Andy chimed in with his usual cheerful tone. "So we make a run through Peotone, then we have more of the same or worse on the other side as we head to Chicago."

"I scouted to the north end." Dwight pointed toward town. "There are some commercial buildings and warehouses there. It appears as though the gangs have already done their business there and the townspeople aren't using that section of town. The only real signs of violence are a Dollar General store that's been looted. Otherwise it's quiet."

"Okay." Vince nodded.

"That's good for us because the local thugs will assume there is nothing left worth taking in that part of town," Dwight said. "I did see a car dealership over a few blocks. It's been hit hard, although it's far enough away that I think we're good. We can shoot through Peotone and then get in one of those warehouses and have a fire and get some shuteye and be back on the road about two a.m."

Vince merely nodded. "Dwight, you're on point. Let's make it happen."

Dwight led them through town quickly and silently to a warehouse that appeared to have been empty long before the current chaos. They got the trucks inside and rigged some simple early warning devices. They chose a watch schedule and cleaned and checked their weapons.

Vince made a meal on a portable Biolite camp stove. "I know it looks funny, but it's light, easy to carry, and can burn almost any debris or sticks around," he said when he saw Andy's raised eyebrow.

Tonight, he was cooking on it. Another time it could warm a tent if needed. Everyone had gear they liked. This was one of those camping and survival items that Vince found useful and easy to carry.

They took turns watching from inside the building so as to minimize their presence and got some sleep. Vince took first watch. At about eleven p.m., Vince tried calling Ellie to no avail.

———

At two in the morning, they got ready for the final run through Chicago to Ellie's. The plan was to leave as soon as they completed some modifications to the trucks. Most of what they needed had been provided by Gus back at French Lick. They used black duct tape to cover most of the lights in World War II blackout out type fashion and removed the bulbs from interior and backup lights. The brake light bulbs were switched for a dull green that could only be seen up close. The parking light bulbs were switched for an infrared bulb that was most easily visible with the night vision goggles.

They rolled out at 3:00 am, staying on Highway 50, or the Governor's Highway as the signs proclaimed for a while. Soon it passed through a nature preserve called Raccoon Grove. It wasn't long after that when the population got denser around where Highway 50 split away from the Governor's Highway heading north. The road they stayed on then became known as Cicero Avenue, a well-known Chicago thoroughfare.

"We need to be on triple alert," Vince cautioned over the radio. "Anything can happen out there, so be very careful and keep your head on a swivel. Take nothing for granted."

Even though it was still dark, dawn was coming. As serene as the open land they were passing through now appeared, it was important to keep in mind how dangerous Cicero would get in a few miles.

When they reached Chicago, they saw roadblocks on side roads from a distance mostly made by cars rolled into the road. There were men standing around fires in fifty-five-gallon drums. They kept moving even though it didn't make sense why Cicero didn't have roadblocks on the main thoroughfare yet and so many side roads did. Vince could only surmise that Cicero acted as a demarcation zone between the turfs of different gangs. A few times as they drove past in the dark, the thugs could hear their engines and would move toward them. Most people couldn't see them at night, and the convoy kept moving. Once, shots were fired toward them, but they didn't return fire because it was clear the shooter didn't know exactly where they were. Their best defense now was that most of the lowlifes were asleep and unaware. Stealth and moving fast was their best friend.

When they passed Lincoln Mall with a Target and a JC Penney nearby, things resembled a war zone. There must have been hundreds of people there. Fires and broken glass were all over the place. They'd probably looted a liquor store nearby, because it didn't appear there was a sober person in sight.

Dwight's urgent voice came over the walkie talkie. *"Follow my lead."* He gunned the engine, honked the horn, and told Andy to blast the radio. When people from the mall noticed Vince and the others, Dwight began shooting out of the windows into the air. Although confused, Vince did the same thing. Soon Vince heard howling and laughter from the mall parking lot, and some of them shot into the air as well.

Dwight came back over the walkie to fill in the others on his strange actions. *"I saw multiple gang colors at the mall, so I thought it was a neutral zone where they don't all know each other. Plus, some of them were pointing at us and we stuck out."*

"Good idea," Vince said. "I doubt they'll go chasing one of their own from the mall when they think we're from another gang just out having fun. That was quick thinking."

It hurt Vince's soul to think of the people who were probably captives and in misery among all those bad people, yet they had a mission and needed to keep driving. According to the map, they were getting close to Ellie's. For the hundredth time this trip, Vince cursed himself for not getting a lay of the land and knowing where his daughter lived long before all of this happened.

As they were headed through a forested area called the "Forest Preserves of Cook County," Vince's SAT phone chimed with a call from Ellie, worrying him because it was getting late in the morning and he and Ellie were not scheduled to talk yet. Vince signaled for Andy and Dwight by tapping his brakes three times to pull off behind him onto a dark side street in the preserve. It appeared that the lowlifes back at the mall had no use for the forest preserve.

ELLIE

Ellie was scared. She didn't try to hide it when she spoke with Vince. She urged him to hurry and told him the gang was closing in, that there had been killings and some neighbors left recently. They no longer had enough people to defend the block.

Vince had always known Ellie to be even keeled and calm. Hearing her scared and at the edge of panic worried him. He needed to stay on plan and get there safely so he could help them. It would be worse if he rushed and got himself into trouble and needed rescue himself.

Ellie shared with Vince that it was the taunts from the gang that got everyone on edge the most. Raheem, the leader, stood at the barricade bragging that his gang had captured the Keselowskis. With delight, he told them that poor Mr. Keselowski didn't make it. However, Mrs. Keselowski and their seventeen-year-old daughter Julie were safe and enjoying *his* protection. He directed the last comment at Malcolm to say they were safer now than with Malcolm.

Malcolm was angry and wanted to go fight his way in to rescue them. It took Ellie, Kate, Liz, and Junior combined to dissuade him. It was sad to see the realization come to Malcolm that he didn't have the skills or firepower to take on a gang. Ultimately, he admitted that he and Junior had only a slight chance of pulling it off. If they tried and failed, Ellie, Kate, Liz, and the others would be left to the same fate.

"The barricades are still in place even though they're not tended now. Everyone pulled back to our house," Ellie relayed. *"Malcolm said to take potshots at the gang members who*

test the barricades. That won't hold them back for long once they figure out no one is at the barricade and we have so few people left. If things get any worse, we'll need to make a run for it at the same time as the others to make it harder for the gang to pick us off. Most of the neighbors left have family somewhere in the city they want to get to."

"I'm only a few hours away. I'm planning to get there sometime later this morning to mid-day. I'll try to get there earlier, but that's a long shot. I have no idea what we'll run into once we get deeper into Chicago."

"Okay," Ellie said. "And Vince?"

"Yeah?"

"Please hurry."

His protective feelings swelled.

Ellie offered to wake Kate, but Vince declined. He was having a hard enough time not running off in haste. He needed to keep his head on straight. "Tell her I'll see her in the morning. Can I speak to Malcolm?"

They hadn't spoken much. Malcolm was protecting his daughter, whom he loved more than life, and Ellie, a woman Vince had loved most of his life. If the truth be told, he still did. The thought of them in danger brought a lump to his throat and sped up his mind in a way that wasn't good for his mission. In combat, it was the man who was able to slow down his thoughts and take it all in and keep a clear mind who would keep his head and survive.

Malcolm described the situation to Vince much the same as Ellie had but went into more detail on his preparations and thought process for defending the block and his family. Both men agreed that he was doing the best he could with what he had. Vince did ask for some visual landmarks to identify as he came into the block. It was important to know where Malcolm thought the gang was hiding and what direction to come in from.

"Where are you?" Malcolm asked.

"We're several miles south of you on Cicero. We're in a forest preserve a little north of Lincoln Mall."

"If you got GPS, don't follow it," Malcolm warned. "It will try and put you on the expressways at several different places. Those expressways are bad enough during normal times in Chicago. I can't even imagine what they're like right now. Cicero won't be much better. At least if you run into trouble here, you can drive down a few side streets to get away. Don't try and fight if you can help it. You'll draw gang bangers like ants to honey."

"Anything else I should be watching for?"

"Dude, you've got a forty-mile gauntlet to run. You better have stones as big as Ellie and Kate think you do and lots of help to make it. Don't get me wrong—I'm rooting for you because we need help badly. Although you've got more to handle than you know."

"You're right, forty miles is quite a trip through hostile territory." Vince's mind

---

flashed back to some of the armored convoys he'd been a part of in Iraq and Afghanistan. In those, he was in armored vehicles with trained troops. Now he had two trucks and three men, counting himself. The hell of it was his reward for making it through was a need to come right back again through the same gauntlet.

Oblivious to Vince's thoughts and obviously thinking about the route, Malcolm said, *"That mall you passed is in a better area of town. That's probably why the gangs went there. You should be okay to move faster for a while. You have two expressways to go under, I-80 and I-57. They're probably okay, but with any overpass like that, you never know. Things could get hairy anywhere along the way. I'd say it will be relatively clear until you pass the Midlothian Turnpike. After that, you want to up your game and be triple alert."*

"Okay," Vince said.

"After Midlothian, you have more places to be wary of, a canal to cross, and another expressway to go under. I'd watch those spots if I was you."

"Thanks," Vince answered, storing away the information.

"You make it through there, then you should be okay for a while longer. Soon after, there is a shopping center on the right called Green Oak. I heard they got hit hard by looters. You might see some of the same as you did at Lincoln Mall. Then more of the same with some of the strip malls a few miles further north. After that, you're going to hit Ford City Mall. Whatever you saw at Lincoln Mall will be peanuts compared to Ford City. If there is any way possible you can go around that, I suggest you do. I have no idea what side streets might be open or blocked. Side streets could be worse than racing through the gauntlet. That choice is on you, man."

"Thanks," Vince said wryly. "You're all good news."

"After Ford City Mall, the road elevates to cross the railroad tracks, and that's another good spot for the gang bangers. Still, you have to get across those tracks. After that, you come to Midway Airport. I have no idea what you'll find there. If you make it through all that, you still have another expressway to go under and another canal to cross. All that does is get you more into the home area of some of these gangs."

Even though Vince was taking a few notes, his memory was sharp. He was visualizing and storing in his mind all that Malcolm said. He didn't like what he was hearing.

"You'll see more shopping centers and movie theaters that will probably be looted or burned. After that, keep an eye out for another expressway, I-294, which you need to go under. When you get close to us, you need to cut over to your right on a side street before you get to Milwaukee Avenue. We're on Kilpatrick in the Irving Hill area. You have the house number."

"I do and I'll be there."

Malcolm responded in a much more somber tone. *"I sure hope so, man. We need you. It's a hell of a trip. If you want to me try and load everyone up and meet you partway, I will. I don't know if we'd make it, though."*

"You all stay put. I'm coming to you. When I get there, we'll be making the same trip out. You can be a hero then."

"Thanks. I don't want to be a hero. I also don't want to be the reason your people or these girls get hurt. I'll do whatever it takes."

As a last thought before he broke connection, Vince asked Malcolm to do one more thing.

"Cut some white bed sheets into strips and tie those to the cars you'll be using. Do the same for the people. Tell them to tie them around their arms or necks. I don't want any mistaken friendly fire casualties if things get dicey in a hurry."

DAVE

Dave resisted the urge to call. More and more he thought of Vince, Ellie, and Kate as his closest family. Although they didn't talk as often as some, they shared a mutual respect, understanding, and love.

Dave and his wife never had children before she died many years ago. Vince was as close to his own child as he could get. He carried his DNA, his last name, and more importantly his spirit. While Vince may not care much about business, in truth neither did Dave. He was just good at it.

It hurt his soul sometimes thinking about his wife even after all these years and the sons and daughters he didn't have. He might have been much less successful in business and so much more successful in life had he been a father. When his mind went down those paths, he got back to work and focused on what a fine man Vince was and that through Kate his family line and legacy would live on.

Dave's brother, also Vince's dad, lived in another state. They had different views, and he could never talk to him like he could Vince, Kate, or even Ellie. Sometimes his brother still acted like the bully from their youth, though he could be polite when he wanted something. It was almost as if his brother resented Dave's success. It was hard for the two of them to talk. He used to have other family members in his generation that he was close to. They had died one by one over the years. That was the worst part about getting old. Most people thought it was declining health or receding hairlines that hurt. His health was fine, and he never cared about his appearance much. What hurt most was seeing friends, family, and peers die off. It was lonely and a constant reminder of his mortality. It forced the thought into his mind of how much closer he was to the end of his timeline on this Earth than the beginning. It also filled him with a sense of urgency to leave something important behind.

As a leader of companies, tens of thousands of employees, and billions of dollars in wealth, Dave wasn't accustomed to waiting. Yet he was smart enough to know when he was meddling and needed to back up and let a plan work itself out. What he could do was beef up security at some plants that were still running and creating essential products to his communities. He could move certain manpower and supplies to other communities and secure locations.

He added extra security people to the Kentucky location and directed Louis to get them anything they needed in terms of supplies. He wanted to make sure they had anything they could possibly need to complete any unfinished work and stock the community.

If all went well, that was where his family and Liz would be headed soon. While he couldn't do much more to help on the ground for this mission, he could make damn sure they had a safe homecoming arranged when they got there.

The next day Dave was catching as much information as he could through the satellite feeds set up for him in the South Park location. The technology people on his staff helped him gather a lot of information, making him probably one of the best informed private citizens in the country at this moment. Yet that wasn't saying much. The blackouts were many and the news fragmented and delayed.

No one would have thought SAT phones would be this unreliable. His tech people couldn't decide if it was due to increased traffic, atmospheric conditions, some type of sabotage, or monitoring by the federal government. Dave was betting on the latter. Now more than ever, the government wanted to know who was saying and doing what. It was clear they weren't making much headway putting down the violence and chaos.

Levi and Louis spent a lot of time with Dave as he went through the news feeds and various personal messages. He valued both of them as a sounding board in different ways, and it was clear the men were frustrated.

Louis liked to have all the information at hand and the ability to reach out to anyone he needed. He didn't like making the hard decisions or else Dave would have put him in charge of something much larger long ago. He was happy to be the Radar O'Reilly to Dave's Colonel Potter. Having late and partial news and not having ready access to all his resources was extremely irritating for Louis.

Levi's frustration was from not being in the field. His good friend was on a mission, and although he was committed to serving Dave, his heart was in the field. If South Park was at risk, Dave could have justified keeping Levi here. As things stood, the only thing holding him back was the belief that he couldn't get Levi anywhere in time to help.

LIZ

As Dave was working on preparations, he got a phone call from Liz. She said she'd been trying a few times a day for the last two or three days to get through.

"I wanted to thank you for the phone and let you know I am safe for the moment at Ellie's place. I'm worried about my family in Kentucky."

"The charter town folks in Kentucky and my nephew made contact with your family. They're safe and doing well," Dave informed her.

Liz expressed her joy at the news yet wasn't shocked. They were a hardy people and didn't live in the big cities. They were survivors.

"Vince offered them a place at the charter town in Kentucky, and they declined the invitation."

"I wouldn't expect anything else."

"Yes, your family insisted they were safe and doing well on the family farm. They wanted to stay there because the violence hasn't come to their part of the country yet and they have the cattle and crops that need tending. I made a deal with them to buy some of what they have through my company."

"Thank you, Dave," Liz said, expressing her gratitude. *"You have a good heart, and you're a man of your word."*

"My nephew Vince was able to convince your grandmother and a couple of nieces to move to the charter town at least part-time, though."

"He what?" Liz exclaimed, astonished.

"Vince convinced them only partially for safety, but mostly because the school is running in the charter town. Your Grandma Jean wanted the kids to have things as normal as possible and continue their education. Living with her at a townhouse in Chartertown Kentucky is safer than trying to commute to their old school or to and from the charter town."

"I can't put into words how much of a weight that removes from me, Dave." It allowed Liz to focus on events at hand and on getting home to Kentucky. After that, they could see what was next.

Dave sensed Liz wasn't ready to hang up yet. "What's on your mind, hon?" he asked in his fatherly way.

"Do you promise to keep what I say to yourself and forget it right after this call?" Liz asked tentatively.

"Sure." Dave's curiosity was piqued.

"It's your nephew. I'm dying of curiosity, and I feel foolish for it. Kate thinks of him as a superhero, which I expect from a daughter. I can tell Ellie does, too. That's not normal for an ex-wife. Heck, even Malcolm is confident Vince is coming to save them, and I don't think those two even know each other that well," Liz poured out in a rush.

"Now I hear he's helped my family. He even talked my grandmother into moving to the Kentucky charter town, even if temporarily. I never thought I'd see anything like that in my life. She won't even visit me in California. It doesn't seem like any one man should be able to do all that. I'm sorry if I'm being disrespectful of your nephew. I can't afford to get my hopes up and be let down."

Dave exhaled with a smile. "You're right not to buy into all the Vince hype. He's a deeply complex individual with more than his fair share of flaws. He hasn't won any gold medals, except a bronze or silver if you count his military service. When he has too much time on his hands, he can drink or be grumpy and brooding. He hasn't made millions with an invention or rose to the ranks of corporate leadership. Don't ever forget he lost Ellie to a divorce, so he has flaws as a husband too. He has just a few loyal friends he's close to."

"Okay?" Liz was clearly confused.

"However, I have never seen a braver man with a truer heart," Dave said. "He will lay down his life for what's right or his fellow man. He has a first responder mentality to run in to trouble when others run out and a kind of supernatural ability to make the right decisions in a split second when bullets are flying. Men follow him with a devotion that he doesn't understand. Women are attracted to him, and they don't know why. His mind is sharp, and his instincts and decisions are sound. I would let him lead any division of my company in a second if he would agree."

"Why don't you or why won't he?" Liz asked.

"His Achilles heel is how his mind works in two areas," Dave said. "The first is that when bullets aren't flying and things aren't chaotic, he feels out of place and drinks or seeks out the next adrenaline rush."

"And the second area?" Liz was clearly intrigued now.

"His guilt," Dave said succinctly. "He remembers every face, every death, and every mission clearly. He may not have a photographic memory, but in this area, it's close. He relives old missions and worries about new ones each night. Over the years, each one of those memories is like another brick in his emotional backpack. He can't unload it, and it partially incapacitates him. Even Ellie couldn't help him with that. He sees the faces of men who died with him in his sleep. He thinks of the missions that didn't succeed as well as he hoped and the people he let down."

"Wow," Liz breathed.

"He will get you out," Dave said confidently. "In that respect, he is nearly a superhero. He is several years older than you, so I shouldn't have to say this, but he is too damaged right now for a nice girl to fall for."

"Dave, seriously!" Liz said, aghast. *"Who could think of falling for a man right now? Besides, he is older than me, and I'm not interested in finding a man right now."*

"Well I'm going to ask the same of you that you did from me," Dave said, wondering if he'd gone too far. "Promise to keep what I say to yourself and forget it right after this call. I have violated some of what Vince and Ellie have told me in confidence by sharing this with you. I trust you and hope you'll forget this when we hang up. I thought you deserved to know is all."

Liz, eager to change the subject, said, *"Thank you, Dave."*

Part Seventeen

VALUE AND COST

"Not all of us are called to die a martyr's death, but all of us are called to have the same spirit of self-sacrifice and love to the very end as these martyrs had."

- Richard Wurmbrand

VINCE

The team fought to make the last few miles to Ellie's home.

There were wrecked and burned-out cars in the road that acted as roadblocks. Vince was sure some of it was done on purpose and some was merely the results of a city tearing itself apart. In either event, they pushed through them when he decided it was the right choice. Other times, they took a detour. He couldn't always put into words what drove the different decisions or what detail he saw that aided his choice. His track record in making the right call was uncannily accurate. This time, it wasn't only a mission that mattered; it was his daughter and ex-wife's lives on the line.

Moving north on Cicero, they encountered places where gangs were fighting each other over the spoils. Occasionally, they saw police or citizens banding together to preserve an island of sanity amidst the chaos. Vince was happy his team hadn't yet come under anyone's special notice. They wanted to avoid fighting and work around it rather than through it. As the day drew on, it became obvious the route up Cicero which would have taken an hour at most a few months ago would take them four, five, or even six now. The problem with taking that much time was the slower they moved, the more likely someone would take notice. The later it got in the day, the more hoodlums would come out on the streets. Twice they returned fire to discourage the attention of someone trying to take what was theirs. Vince's paramount concern was saving the vehicles and making good time. The men with him were strong and could fight their way to Ellie's on foot if they needed to. Yet the goal was not only to get there, but to get everyone out of Chicago and back to

Kentucky safely. Ellie, Kate, and the others couldn't fight their way through territory like this on foot the way Vince and his team could.

As they moved further north, they were forced to fight more. They soon fell into a routine of plan A and plan B. Plan A was to rush the obstacle or attackers fast with the vehicles in line and pouring lead. Plan B was riskier and amounted to a dismounted cavalry option when they found a hard blockage. In that situation, they'd find a hiding place to park the vehicles, behind a building or in an alley. Usually it would be Andy that would guard the vehicles while Vince and Dwight would move up silently. The plan wasn't to kill them all or take ground. It was merely to unleash a sudden unexpected hell on the hoodlums and make them scatter. The team needed to keep moving north and clearing a path.

It was close to two in the afternoon before they got close to Ellie's block. The landmarks Malcolm gave him were good, and the map confirmed it. Still, he didn't want to go racing in to Kilpatrick Avenue without getting a lay of the land. They found a back alley about a block west of Ellie's home where they could hide the vehicles in the shadows of an alley between two older homes. Most of the houses on this block were burned out or deserted.

Vince dismounted and worked his way closer to get a better view. A cold chill ran down his spine when he saw several gang members firing into the front of what he was sure was Ellie and Malcolm's home. A flash of panic raced through his body as he worried about his daughter and ex-wife. He forced himself to take a deep breath. It was hard to keep his cool and not rush in. What convinced him there was more time was the high rate of return fire coming from inside. The criminals had time and were enjoying inflicting terror as well as softening up the defenders.

Vince decided not to go for a full-on assault right this second. He instructed Andy and Dwight to conceal themselves in sniper nests and be ready for his command. All three men were using simple walkie talkies with ear buds and could communicate any strategy adjustments. The advantage of working with men like Andy and Dwight was that they were professionals and only needed a word or two to understand a change in plan.

Vince took a chance and tried calling Ellie on the SAT phone, miraculously getting through on the second try. It was Kate who answered. Vince was overjoyed at hearing her voice and knowing she was okay, at first. Kate spoke rapidly, her voice rushed and tinged with panic as she related how the gang had sauntered up with their demands. They were led by Raheem and followed by his sneering brother Malik.

LIZ

The ring of the phone startled Liz.

She could hear Kate's side of the conversation with her dad, and a ray of hope poked through the terror they'd been living through facing the gang. She didn't understand why so many other people trusted him so thoroughly to make things right. When they spoke of Vince, their body language conveyed a trust that was infectious. Liz listened to the pride and confidence Dave had in his nephew when he spoke of him and the adoration in Kate's voice when she talked about her dad. While it was natural enough that a daughter would feel that way about her father, Vince's ex-wife also still cared for and trusted him to save them. Even Ellie's new husband Malcolm trusted Vince to help keep his family safe.

Under other circumstances, this would be a man she'd want to know better. Not in a romantic way, but as a man. Liz had always liked no nonsense, confident people who got things done and didn't need accolades or seek attention.

Liz stopped listening to Kate's side of the conversation with her dad. Even Kate was partially distracted at this point, and her words drifted off. They were all rapt spectators to the demands and shouts between the gang leader and Malcolm.

Raheem spoke from the cover of cars in front of Malcolm's home. "Send out the guns, women, and food and I'll let the men live."

The other survivors from the block were crowded into Malcolm's house and heard the exchange. Liz was scared when a couple of the other men looked around the room as if considering the offer; she could see a moment of terror on Kate's face as she saw the same looks.

Malcolm defiantly yelled out, "Raheem, I know who you are, and I know Malik too. You are a no-good son of a bitch. You ain't getting nothing but a world of hurt if you keep coming at us! Any man that hurts me or mine won't live long. You *all* know me!"

Raheem didn't see that when Malcolm spoke those words, he was glaring directly at his neighbors in his own home. "Raheem, this whole city and possibly this whole country's gone to hell. It's your world now. It would be a shame to die here on this block right near where you grew up and miss out. Leave us be!"

Malik responded with a hail of bullets before Raheem could get a word out. The speech might have worked on Raheem. Malik was plain crazy. After the barrage, a couple of people were bleeding with scratches. None appeared to be hit badly.

The only person whose injury was more serious was old Mr. Goldberg. He was the son of Holocaust survivors and was born not long after the war. Ellie had told Liz how his house was kept up so fastidiously. Liz and Ellie helped Mr. Goldberg wrap a pressure dressing around his side, where he was bleeding. He insisted it wasn't that bad.

After the barrage, Kate purposefully laid the phone down so the call wouldn't disconnect and approached Malcolm with an expression of confidence that hadn't been there a few minutes earlier. Liz sensed that things were about to change in their favor.

Malcolm called for most of their attention while a few still fired random shots to keep the gang's attention. "Vince is only a little ways down the block," he said hurriedly. "His plan is to hit the gang hard to disperse as many of them as possible. Without doing that, the gang could hurt many of us when we go out. Vince needs most of the gang in the front yard so they can hit them hard in crossfire both from the house and behind."

"Who is Vince? Why should we trust him?" one of the neighbors asked.

Ellie's face got tight. Kate seemed about the burst with anger. Malcolm stepped in the middle and just said, "He's the cavalry."

While Malcolm spoke to Vince, Kate and Ellie began cutting up white bedsheets and handing them out, explaining the purpose for them as Vince had directed. Everyone began talking in a rush, putting forth different ideas to get the gang in the front yard.

Then the front door opened.

ELLIE

Ellie picked up the phone. *"Vince..."* Before he could respond, he heard Ellie's frantic voice saying, *"Oh my God, he's going outside!"*

Vince wasn't ready to act and wasn't sure what Ellie's shout meant. All Vince could see from his vantage after hearing Ellie's words was an older man holding his bleeding side walk onto the lawn in front of Ellie and Malcolm's home. He held up a white handkerchief speckled with blood from his coughs.

"Don't shoot." He turned back to the house, raised a single hand. "Stop shooting."

Everyone paused. No one on either side knew quite what to do. It was obvious no one planned for this. Some of the gang members came out to see what he wanted. Others held back, suspicious of a trap. Soon the old man was standing in the front yard near the cars at the curb surrounded by half of the gang. They gathered around him, cutting off the view from the house and Vince both. None of them could hear what was being said.

Andy and Dwight reported in by radio that they were loaded and ready. Vince instructed them to hold their position until he could decide what was going on.

There was a commotion in the middle of the group, and gunshots rang out. Vince was still confused as to who the old man was and who was shooting at whom. He dared not interrupt if this was some scheme by the defenders.

Ellie looked on in horror. Mr. Goldberg walked through the front door waving what was once an elegant monogrammed white handkerchief, now speckled with blood.

He called for Raheem. As he did, many of the gang circled him. Raheem approached, blocked from those in the house by his own men. Raheem held an unusually large gold-plated handgun to Mr. Goldberg's head. Ellie had once seen Vince scoff at a similar one in a gun shop as a showpiece. It was a Desert Eagle and was comical at the end of Raheem's long, slender arm.

Mr. Goldberg stood tall and said defiantly, "You don't want to shoot me yet, son. If you do, you won't find my gold coins."

"What gold, old man? You ain't got no gold or you wouldn't be living here," Malik said with a sneer, while Raheem peered at him speculatively.

Mr. Goldberg ignored Malik and stared back at Raheem defiantly.

Raheem lowered the gun an inch and spoke in a low, measured way that was the opposite of Malik's maniacal rant. "You'll give me the gold, guns, women, food, and anything else I want if you want to live."

"What is he saying?" Liz said to the group in general as she peered out the window, her voice betraying her distress. *"I can't hear him. Why are they all getting around him? Can't we go help him?"*

"Mr. Raheem, I am an old man. I am injured and will die soon one way or the other. I like to think I'm a good man. I know this world cannot rebound or thrive when good men stand aside and watch bad men flourish. I've lived a long life with the stories of what it was like when we last allowed bad men to flourish." He paused to get his breath and wipe more blood from his mouth. "You, Mr. Raheem, are not as mean and scary as Hitler. Then again, I'm not as good or heroic as a man would have to be to face down a Hitler. Nevertheless, I can do for you." Mr. Goldberg bent over and coughed up more blood, his voice becoming little more than a whisper. All Raheem could hear was the word "gold."

As Raheem bent down to hear better and Mr. Goldberg was fighting to stand again, they came together. Mr. Goldberg wrapped one arm around Raheem's shoulder in an effort to keep from falling. With the other, he pulled a .38 Special revolver that had been a gift from his father who had survived the Holocaust. He shoved it into Raheem's belly and pulled the trigger repeatedly until it was empty and both men, the good and the bad, collapsed to the ground.

Had anyone been able to hear Mr. Goldberg's last words, they would have heard him say, "My people will never be victims again."

VINCE

The gang erupted after the gunshots.

Someone was getting the bad end of that bargaining session. Vince assumed it was the old man he saw leave Ellie's home. He was still unsure if this was the time to act. He wanted to take his cue from the people inside the house. It was hearing Malcolm's primal yell that made the decision for him. Malcolm saw the sweet old man go down. He didn't know that Mr. Goldberg shot Raheem. He only saw the gang fall upon the old man with guns and knives in a fury. Malcolm's own buried rage at being forced from his job, home, and city came boiling to the top. He opened up with the old pump shotgun that sat under the counter of his dad's shop for so many years. He didn't know if he hit anything. He didn't care. He only knew he needed to fight back. The others took his lead and fired into the gang as well.

That was all Vince needed to see. He directed his team to open fire. When Vince's men opened up on the unprotected flank of the gang, the damage was devastating. Some tried to return fire on Vince's position. Then the enraged people from the house led by Malcolm poured out and began firing at point-blank range. All the targets left standing in the open were wearing their gang colors. None of them, except the bloodied, ravaged corpse of the old man, had the white sheets tied to them that Vince requested.

After most of the gang was killed or routed, Vince searched for his ex-wife and daughter. When he saw them alive and safe, his knees shook and nearly buckled with relief.

It was that distraction that allowed Malik and a few others that had been hiding behind a car to make their dash for safety.

When it was over, Malcolm wanted to bury Mr. Goldberg properly. Vince insisted they didn't have time. They needed to honor Mr. Goldberg's sacrifice by getting the people out to safety. Malcolm did speak the words from John 15:13 over Mr. Goldberg's body even though it wasn't his religion; he thought the sweet old man wouldn't mind. "No one has greater love than this. To lay down one's life for his friends."

Then Malcolm wrapped Mr. Goldberg in a sheet and picked him up as sweetly as a father might carry his newborn child and put him to bed one last time in his neat little home on Kilpatrick Avenue.

LIZ

When Malcolm gave that primal scream in anger at Mr. Goldberg's death, it galvanized the others. They began shooting and poured out of the house to finish off the gang.

Liz wasn't able to move. This shouldn't be happening. They needed her. She was part of the team. There were no police to help and no one to call. It was simply their group against the bad guys, an age-old tale of good versus evil. While her mind was able to reconcile that what they were doing was right, something in her chest insisted this was wrong. As those thoughts were going through her mind, she could see the gang being killed a few feet in front of her while her body froze in place.

When it was over, she followed the rest of the group out of the house in a daze, an unfired revolver hanging limp in her hand. Seeing poor Mr. Goldberg's frail, ravaged body lying in the small yard made something turn cold inside her. It was resolve. She had seen Jennifer and now Mr. Goldberg die horrible deaths while she'd been helpless to stop it. As she saw his body, she reflected that he had known what needed doing and he'd gone out and stood for something that was right and gave his life for them.

That resolve hardened in her chest. She would no longer be a victim. She whispered the words of Maimonides that she had once practiced for a play: "*The risk of a wrong decision is preferable to the terror of indecision.*"

She would not be a spectator in her life again.

Part Eighteen

STORMS ABATE

"If your actions inspire others to dream more, learn more, do more and become more, you are a leader."

- John Quincy

VINCE

Adams

Vince looked into each of their faces.

He saw the same looks he'd seen dozens of times before, a mixture of hope and uncertainty. These were people who had lost direction and confidence and needed someone to provide those things. They needed someone to step up. They didn't know that when they gave over to someone to provide guidance and hope, they also laid a heavy burden at that person's feet. The results of good decisions and bad, and who lived or died, now resided with the leader. For a conscientious person, that burden was heavy. Every loss or injury to the people you led stayed with you for a lifetime. It was a leader's version of PTSD.

Vince thought he was done with all that. He was content to go to the office and do his nine to five work. The memories of people he'd failed in war and in his personal life was enough for a lifetime. He didn't want more.

He also knew he would carry the burden of this mission's successes or failure whether he led or not. If he gave them over to someone else who failed or couldn't do what he could do, then he was just as at fault as if he'd led. He was a good leader and made good choices. He wasn't perfect. No man could be.

Vince steeled his resolve and took a moment to peer back at each one of them. He saw a cocktail of relief, hope, concern, and worry etched in their faces. Every face was different, yet all had one thing in common. They needed hope and leadership. Vince knew that look. This was his time to step forward. He didn't do it with pride. He didn't do it with elation, fear, or even uncertainty. He did it with a type of weight that laid heavy on the soul. From the next moment on, their fate was in his hands. Maybe not totally and maybe they didn't even feel that way consciously, but he knew it. If someone got hurt or died, a piece of him would die too. When he took on that weight, it would feel like he was walking with a rucksack loaded with a hundred pounds of rocks. In reality, he'd been carrying that weight since he began this trip. It was only now as he looked in their faces that he knew it soul deep. There was no turning back. Only when they made it home safely would he be able to lay down that burden.

If any didn't make it, that weight could never totally be put down. There were rocks in his emotional rucksack he'd been carrying for years that he would never put down. Somehow, someway, you got used to it. Or else.

Vince stood a bit taller and addressed the group. "Folks, we need to get moving. We have them on the run for now. They'll be back with friends for sure. Others will have heard the gunshots too. They'll be like scavengers coming for scraps or spoils. Malcolm, I can fit a few folks in our vehicles. Do you have more vehicles ready?"

"Yes. I've got a minivan and an Expedition parked out back. They're partly loaded and ready to run. With what you have and those, we should be good."

Vince nodded to Malcolm and spoke to the group. "Does anyone else have anything to load? I want to be on the road in less than ten minutes. We're in good shape, and we're going to get through this together. I'm going to do something that's a little risky, but it's our best chance. I expect it to work because we will do it fast and unexpectedly. We're going out now in daylight, right back out the way we came in."

People murmured and shuffled nervously.

"You can't stay here. Malcolm has told me some of you want to go your own way. I want you to know you're all welcome to come with us. In either event, you need to trust me that this place is going to be crawling with crooks and killers inside an hour. Whichever way you're going we need to be long gone before they come back."

"We're with you, Vince," Malcolm said. "We can be packed in five minutes. What's your plan?"

"I want to make a serious run at getting south of the city before it gets dark to an old warehouse district we stayed in last night. We'll rest there for a few hours and be back on the road by two or three in the morning. I can go through more of the wheres and whys later. For now, we need to be away from here. Get what you need, folks. Take only what you can carry. Focus on guns, ammo, and food. If you can't hold it in your arms, we don't have room for it."

Kate stayed back a step out respect for her father. When he finished, she ran into his arms and hugged him tightly. "I want to ride with you, Daddy!"

Vince held her for a moment, savoring the feel of his daughter in his arms, safe for the moment. He leaned back, his eyes locked on hers. "No, I need you to ride with your mom and Malcolm. They need a good shot like you with them. Your mom will worry if you're not with her. Plus, I'll be lagging back a bit to check on a few things."

Kate's voice rose, and there was a tinge of panic building in it. "Daddy, don't! I know what you're going to do! You're going to stay back and fight anyone who tries to hurt us. It doesn't always have to be you! You don't always have to be the one who saves people and fixes things. Let one of the other men do it! They will. I know they will!"

Vince hugged her, his eyes damp, and his heart aching. "Yes, it does have to be me, honey. It's my job, and I need to do it. I don't know why. I expect I'll know when it's someone else's turn. For now, it's me, and we both know it. You know me better than anyone in this world. We're a lot alike. But hey, Squirrel, I'm hard to kill. I'll be there to tease you before you know I'm gone. I'll only be a bit. Now don't worry, and go help your mom."

ELLIE

Ellie observed her ex-husband from a distance of feet and time.

She couldn't help feeling a sense of guilt on many levels. Guilt because Malcolm was a good man and yet she was so relieved to see her ex. Vince was a man who got things done and always knew where to be or what to do when he was needed. *Well, at least he was good in life or death situations,* she thought with a wry smile.

It was the normal day to day stuff in which he wasn't so good. Darn it, though, if he wasn't a man's man, the kind women were drawn to. He was still attractive in a rugged way, she admitted to herself as long as she was indulging in these thoughts.

Then she had the other type of guilt. Had she tried hard enough? Vince was a good man in his own way. He could be cold and distant, even moody at times. Why couldn't he tell that a woman needed more than that? In her self-doubt, she wondered if he needed more help than she'd been able to give. Maybe she wasn't able to learn what he needed. She wondered for a moment if she quit too soon. They had tried for twelve years. Well, *she* had tried for twelve years.

It was over and done, and they needed to deal with the here and now.

LIZ

Liz was impressed with Vince. Not in a romantic way, but in the way that a man can make a woman feel safe and protected.

Having been raised in a rural Kentucky family, she knew his type. Vince wasn't pretty like the men in Hollywood. His muscles weren't bulky and defined like the models always ready for a photo shoot. He had a few days' beard growth, mussed hair, and a faraway look in his eyes that spoke of a heavy weight on his mind and haunted memories. He exhibited confidence and a protective nature about him that women were drawn to and men followed. Liz observed the group one by one and saw that both the old and young felt more protected, confident, and hopeful than before he showed up. The men were more assured in their step. They had a plan and a leader. While some men rose to the occasion when a leader was needed, others preferred being the strong arm of implementation of another man's plan. It was clear to see that Vince was born to lead and these men gained strength and confidence by having a man to follow. It wasn't that Malcolm wasn't a good man and a strong man; it was only that he didn't inspire confidence the way Vince did.

Liz moved to get her things in order. As a successful actress, it was her job to be observant of human nature. Who knew when she might choose to use something she learned in a role? She once worked with an older actress who had been raised in a rural town much like Liz. When the discussion turned to the normal type of man in Hollywood, they both snickered. It was that older actress who used a line about men that always stuck in Liz's mind. *"Masculinity is not something given to you, but something you gain. And you gain it by winning small battles with honor."*

Liz thought Vince had that kind of masculinity.

LEVI

"Levi, I know this is something you need to do. I've grown to value your input and insights. We both know you'd rather be in the field with Vince, not back here guarding an old man, though."

Dave and Levi were enjoying a drink on the massive log veranda with a commanding view of the South Park Valley. Dave didn't smoke, and although he never drank to excess, he did enjoy an occasional glass of Kentucky bourbon. Today he was drinking Wild Turkey Rare Breed. Louis had a couple of things to finish up and then would be along soon to join them if he was able.

"You're safe here, Mr. Cavanaugh. We have a well-trained group of men and women. This valley is very remote, and the citizens are good people, almost to the last man." Levi spoke as if stating a rehearsed case. "Vince is my friend, and I don't make many. I think he needs my help."

Levi paused, appreciating the serenity in a way that only a man accustomed to violence can. When things got crazy and people were screaming or crying and he couldn't get a breath of clean air, this would be what he longed for. He continued as much for himself as an explanation for Dave. "Whether he does or doesn't, it wouldn't feel right to me if I didn't try."

"I understand that."

"I respect decisions of leadership," Levi said. "I'll stay here if that's what you think is best." It was obvious he didn't want to stay, despite a deep sense of duty.

Dave waved the hand that held the drink in a motion to dismiss Levi's statement. "I don't know how much help you can be to him this late in the game, although you can be there to guard the gate, so to speak, when he gets close to home. Vince is like a son to me. I want him safe too."

"If you can help me get the flight approved, it's a quick trip there and back. You won't even notice I'm gone," Levi said in a rush.

"I knew you would ask. I've already checked into it and made some plans. Most flights nationwide are grounded with all the chaos and sabotage. However, I still have some strings to pull, and with Louis's help, I have."

"That's great. I'll get my things together. Where do I go?" Levi responded with growing enthusiasm.

"I gave direction to have two of the planes that can handle shorter runways moved up to the Leadville-Lake County Airport here in the mountains. You can use one of those. Take whatever you think you might need in terms of men or supplies."

"I don't think I've been there," said Levi.

"If there was a road over the mountain, it would be only a few miles away," Dave said. "Unfortunately, you have an hour or more drive around to where you have a pass to get through the mountains and back up to Leadville."

"Why shouldn't I just head down to Colorado Springs?" Levi asked.

"Even though the chaos there is better than most cities right now, it's still bad. Also, that airport is more tightly controlled than Leadville-Lake. I have the pull to make sure you're not forced to land, although not enough to get Colorado Springs opened up for you. You're a very competent man, Levi. I have no doubt you can make it into and out of any city in the country. Don't ever forget to arrange for all the details and not rush into things. I have plans for you."

Levi held Dave in such great esteem he wasn't hurt. He didn't want to let him down.

"You haven't done anything wrong, Levi," Dave said, sensing Levi's disappointment. "I know you're in a hurry to help your friend. You know your own skills. The things going on are not formidable enough to worry you. I can't put my planes, crews, and support people in danger, though."

"Thanks, boss. I really appreciate it." Levi stood to refill their glasses.

"Don't thank me. You're going to help my nephew, who is the closest family I have left. Besides, you've become like family to me as well. Take care of yourself, too. Don't take unnecessary risks." Dave reached over to pat Levi on his massive forearm.

"If Colorado Springs is that bad, I don't suppose I can get into Louisville, either," Levi said, thinking aloud.

"Louisville is a mess for sure. My plan was always to use the private airport in Madison, Indiana, to support the Carrollton site, except now I'm getting reports of gangs in Madison. I don't trust sending a plane in there. Louis hasn't been able to get any replies from our contacts on that side of the river or with the airport there."

"I'm willing to take the chance. I can lead a team to clean up that airport if you think it makes sense," Levi volunteered.

"It's not a risk I think is wise right now for either you or my plane." Dave chuckled. "Louis and I spoke. We think that flying into a small airport in Springfield, Kentucky, will be our best bet. It's rural enough to be safe, and it has a long, paved runway and other facilities we'll need. The problem is we will be flying in there blind. The pilots have never been there, and none of my people know anyone there."

"I'm willing."

"I can see your enthusiasm, and I know you want to go try to help your friend." Dave smiled, showing the crinkle lines around his eyes. "So that's what we'll do. The manager at the airport has returned my message. He's willing to trade the facilities' use and fuel for supplies and gold coins. You'll be on your own after that. Getting to the Carrollton site from Springfield won't be easy. I don't recommend going through any of the larger cities. If you head north on Highway 55, you can get there with some twists and turns. That route will take you near Shelbyville, Kentucky. Vince has a good family friend in that area. My hope was to get him to guide you through back roads. I haven't been able to get in touch with him yet, though. I'll give you his name and number so if we don't get in touch with him you can try when you're on the ground. He lives in Todd's Point, Kentucky, which doesn't even show up on many of the maps. His name is Greg Simpson."

Levi nodded. "I've heard Vince mention him."

"Louis and I will keep trying to get ahold of him. If we can, or you're able to when you land, that's the perfect person to be your guide through the back roads that are safer. I'll give you his address as well in case you can hook up with him or need a safe place along the route to hole up."

"That's good, thanks."

"I'll have Louis keep trying e-mail and text messages to reach Greg while you're flying. If we get a hold of him, we'll let you know."

"Thanks again," Levi said, eager to be on his way.

"I know you already know this, Levi, but once you land, the SAT phones are very iffy. While you're in the air, the communications to the plane are more solid."

"Well, here's to a successful trip." Levi held up his glass to Dave. It was clear he was done talking and wanted to get moving. "When can I leave?"

"Now if you want. Get your stuff together and have one of the men drive you to Leadville. Louis sent instructions to the crew to fuel up and have the plane checked out mechanically earlier today. It should be done by the time you get there."

Levi was already headed toward the door, his refreshed drink forgotten. Even in haste, the big man moved quietly and catlike. He covered the steps two at a time and was already out of sight when he said almost as an afterthought, "Thanks again, boss. I'll be back soon." His voice was much more full of energy now. This was Levi's element and what he loved.

Part Nineteen

LEAVING HOME

"*A man with character strengths is all that a woman not only admires, but feels deep respect for.*"

- Unknown

ELLIE

As she loaded the last of her plastic bins in the minivan, Ellie glanced back at her home with some nostalgia and remorse.

Although she hadn't been here long, she loved the home and enjoyed her new life in Chicago. Kentucky was her old home. It was filled with mixed emotions. Chicago was her new life and held such promise for the next chapter in her journey with all the options for shopping, theater, restaurants, and the arts.

Ellie's life with Malcolm in Chicago had been more than she expected or hoped for. It didn't feel as if it was only the home she was leaving; it was her new life, and it was the abandonment of her fresh start and a retreat to her old life in Kentucky.

All these thoughts were in her mind as she hugged Malcolm. "Do you think we'll ever come back?"

"Sure we will, baby," Malcolm said in an effort to reassure her. "Don't give up. This is only for a little while. We'll return and fix it all up, good as new."

Something in Malcolm's voice didn't convince Ellie he totally believed what he was saying. "I feel so guilty," Ellie confessed. "I've been so focused on myself I haven't given much thought to how you feel. This is your home and where you grew up. You must be devastated."

"I'm not convinced I won't be back. I don't have time for that now. If I thought I'd never be back, I might feel differently."

"I hope you're right," Ellie said as she leaned her head into his chest.

"Chicago has changed a lot since I was young. It's not the same city. I haven't felt as much at home since my dad died. My family is with you and Kate now and

making sure you two are safe and happy. After that, I'll worry about my home."
Malcolm spoke with a sincerity that convinced her he meant it. It made her heart
swell.

For Ellie, it wasn't only the uncertainty of gangs and violence she would be
driving into; it was a life she chose to leave behind in Kentucky. It wasn't a terrible
life, but it was one that she thought she'd put behind her. Now she had to pick at
the scab and open that emotional wound again. She sighed and climbed into
the van.

As if he could sense her thoughts, Malcolm squeezed her arm and put the
minivan into gear. She exhaled. Things would work out. They always did somehow,
someway, although rarely the way you'd planned.

VINCE

Vince put Andy and Dwight on point with instructions to make it as far south on Cicero as they could. The goal was to get back to the area they spent last night in as fast as possible. If they needed to stop along the way, the first choice was the wooded preserve.

If they made it to the building they stayed in last night and anyone was around to see them enter, he instructed them keep going until they found a safer, more deserted place. This all needed to be done before dark. For experienced operators, moving under the cover of darkness was preferred. However, with two cars of civilians and not enough night vision, Vince judged the risk too great.

"What are you going to do, boss?" Andy asked.

"I'm going to hang back and check some things out. I'll catch up to you all. Don't be surprised if from time to time you see me and then you don't. My plan is to stop occasionally and make sure our back trail is clear."

"Okay." Andy figured there was more to Vince's plan but didn't ask.

"If you don't see me, you can reach me by radio. Let's try and keep that to a minimum. I don't know who might be listening."

"Sure, boss. Do you think there will be more trouble from behind than in front?"

"I don't know. I have a weird feeling about that gang. Call it a hunch."

Andy nodded. "Your hunches have been good so far. Let's keep trusting them."

"I need to find a good spot and make sure I'm not being watched," Vince told him. "When I do, I'll duck into a dark alley or something. I want to set up a nasty surprise for anyone following us. If I'm wrong, this will just be a waste of time. If my hunch is right, this is a chance I can't miss. I know your planned route. Anyone following us doesn't. That means I have the upper hand for now. I can't afford to waste this opportunity."

"That's true," said Dwight. "But why not let me do it?"

"I know you could." Vince smiled in appreciation for Dwight's offer. "This is my hunch, and I need to follow it through. I can hurt anyone following us pretty good and perhaps permanently if I find a good ambush spot. I might even get myself a little bit of shut eye while I wait."

"Roger that," both men said in unison.

"I want to be rested tonight so I can check some things out where we camp while the others are sleeping."

While many people would think it an odd plan to set up an ambush and then find a spot for a nap, Andy and Dwight had quickly learned to trust Vince and went with it.

Andy spoke for both men. "Okay, boss, don't hesitate to call if you need us. We want to get you out alive too. We're a team and don't plan to go home short a man."

LIZ

Liz overheard the conversation between Vince and his men. A part of her wanted to ride with Vince, yet she was still scared and remembered her inaction in the fire-fight a few minutes earlier.

"Vince, I need a minute of your time, and please hear me out before you reply." When Vince turned to her, she experienced the weight of his gaze as his ice cold blue eyes seemed to bore through her. "I heard what you said to your men and what Kate said to you earlier. I know what you're planning. I'm pretty sure that doing that alone is not a good idea. This group has been more focused and confident since you rode in. Do you think it's a good idea to leave us to our own devices so soon?" Liz meant it purely as a question. It came out more challenging than she intended.

"It needs to be done."

"I expected that. I assume you don't want to put us at more risk by keeping one of your men with you. I know I'm not a good enough shot to help you. I insist that you take my bodyguard Junior with you, though. He's good and a former Marine or something. I'm sure he can help. I'll feel better if you do."

When Vince started to shake his head and reply, Liz held up her hand to stop him. "I'm not done yet. I've thought this through, and I know I'm right. I won't take no for an answer."

They locked eyes for a moment.

"I can be difficult when I don't get what I want. You don't have time for a spoiled Hollywood actress, so please just go with it."

Vince let out his breath and smiled. Liz smiled back and gave a snort that was mostly from relief. The only argument he could come up with was, "What if he doesn't want to join me in this? He could get killed. Besides, his mission is to protect you, not me. You're the *star*," Vince said in a way that could have been interpreted as a sneer, but Liz recognized a playful banter in his tone.

"If he doesn't want to go, then I'm going with you even if I have to walk."

"I'd say with you as his boss, he'll go. I can't imagine how you'd make him feel if he doesn't." Vince turned to walk away.

"What do you mean by that?" Liz asked, trotting to catch up to Vince. She couldn't tell if they were still bantering. Liz felt like she should be angry. She did feel a little hurt like she'd been dismissed and belittled by Vince when he walked away.

Vince was impressed by Liz. She was strong, pretty, determined, and wanted to do what was right. Even so, he wasn't a people person and didn't know how to talk to a lady like her. Besides, he had bigger things on his mind at the moment. He got angry at himself for beginning to banter and flirt and get distracted. As soon as he realized it, he stopped and moved his mind back to the mission.

While he recognized the value in taking another man with him, he didn't have time to flirt, especially with a pretty girl right in front of his ex-wife, daughter, and men during a mission.

LEVI

The pilot of the private jet called for Levi to come forward.

"We have a message from corporate."

"Go ahead," Levi said, kneeling to fit his huge frame in the door to the cockpit.

"The boss's assistant, Louis, asked me to pass on that they received a message from Greg Simpson. He will be at the Springfield airport when we land."

"How will I know him?" Levi asked.

The pilot shrugged. "I don't know. They didn't tell me anything specific. They only said to tell you to keep an eye out for an older farmer named Greg Simpson."

"How long until we land?"

"About forty-five minutes, give or take."

"What are your instructions after you drop me off?"

"We have a few supplies for the locals and some for you and the Carrollton site. It's not much because we were told that you didn't know what type of transportation you'd have."

"Nice," Levi commented affably. "I didn't know you had room for much cargo space."

"This plane was built more for passengers. It's been modified some to give up a few seats for a little more cargo space. There are a couple of cases they told me to make sure got into your hands personally. They appear to be gun cases from their shape and size."

"You have my curiosity up! So, after you drop me, do you head back to Colorado?"

"My instructions are to fuel up if it tests out clean, then I have some things to take to the Texas charter town location."

"Texas, huh?" Levi said, now very curious.

"It's mostly coins to pay workers with and a couple of other cases that could be guns or whatever. They told me the Texas site is well behind the Kentucky one in progress and supplies. I heard that both the workers and some local people who have supplies are responding much better to precious metal-type currency."

———

When they landed, the buildings and runway of the small country airport gave the impression of stepping back in time. The runway was a long double strip of pavement. The building and tower could have been something out of the seventies. When Levi stepped off the plane, there was indeed a man dressed like a Midwestern farmer waiting for him. Based on what Vince had told him and the description passed through the pilot, this must be Greg. He was still in good shape despite being in his early sixties and graying a bit on top.

Greg approached Levi with a big smile on his face and stuck out his hand. "You're not from around here, are you?" he asked and chuckled at his own joke.

Levi grinned and shook Greg's hand. "I'm Levi. Vince told me about you. It's good to meet you."

"I'm sure none of what Vince said was good. Still, any friend of Vince's is a friend of mine. They said you needed a ride or guide, and here I am," Greg responded with enthusiasm to match Levi's.

"I'm trying to get to the Carrollton charter town location. I'm sure I could get there on my own, although it will be so much easier with a guide. With most of the country fighting and stealing from each other right now, I appreciate your help."

"Naw, it ain't that bad here," Greg said. "I'm happy to take you there, though. The missus is with me and her little dog too, if that's okay with you?"

"It's your truck," Levi responded. "If you're sure it's fine and we have room, I have a few other cases to load."

"Sure we do. We can put your stuff in the back. Besides, I wanted to take the missus to see that charter town anyways. I didn't want to leave her home alone while I came here."

"What about your farm? Won't people steal from you while you're gone?"

"I doubt it," Greg said. "I have some friends from my church group staying at the place. Plus, it's not the country folk we worry about. It's the city people. By the time they get out to my place, they're more tired, cold, and hungry than dangerous."

"Don't they try to steal your cattle?" Levi pressed.

Greg hooted. "Well, heck no," he said, drawing out his words as if Levi just asked the dumbest question. "They're all on foot by the time they get to the country. None of them know how to pull a trailer or herd cattle into it. They mostly walk right up to my cows with a gun or knife. I could stop 'em, but I figure it's more fun to watch and better they learn a lesson the hard way."

"What's the hard way?"

"My cattle are all crossed with Texas longhorns. Not only can they protect themselves, they're aggressive about it. I've seen 'em run off a person or two. It won't surprise me if they kill a few before this is all over," Greg said with amusement dancing in his eyes.

Levi couldn't do much more than nod and smile.

"I heard the restaurant over to the Carrollton site was still open," said Greg. "I figured I'd take the missus out to dinner while we're out and about. We might stay a day or two if you have room for us and then head home."

Levi smiled at Greg's infectious good humor. "Of course there's room for you. But the whole country is tearing itself apart and you're worried about taking your wife out to dinner?"

"Well, you can't let things get you down. I'm a believer in God. He will take me when He's ready. There's no reason to be foolhardy, but you can't live in fear, either."

"We can get going then as soon I load these cases. Do you know a good route?" Levi asked.

"It's all pretty safe along the route we'll take. I'll avoid most of the bigger towns to be on the safe side, though. It should only take us a few hours."

"Sounds good. Are you armed?"

"I carry an old double-barreled coach gun I've owned for years. I'm sure that will be plenty."

Part Twenty

GAUNTLET

"*Success is not final, failure is not fatal: it is the courage to continue that counts.*"

- Winston Churchill

ELLIE

Malcolm drove the red minivan away from home on Kilpatrick Avenue, heading south on Cicero Avenue.

He followed the black vehicle ahead of him, a four-door sport truck. Malcolm made sure to stay a couple of car lengths behind as he'd been instructed. He and Ellie were aghast at the damage, burned-out buildings, and general eerie feel of the city.

"I've never seen Chicago this quiet," Ellie said in a hushed voice. "I would never have imagined it could be like this."

"It's not right," Malcolm said. "This town has always been bustling with activity for well over a hundred and fifty years." The area was so different with all the burned-out cars and broken windows.

Ellie shuddered. "I keep watching the buildings and homes and wondering which ones have good people who are hiding and which ones have bad people who are watching at us like prey."

Malcolm kept his eyes moving from side to side to make sure no one was approaching the vehicle. His mind was working overtime, thinking about the fate of their city while keeping his head on a swivel and watching for threats as they fled it. "The good and bad of it isn't as simple as it was a few weeks ago. There are good people doing bad things because they were unprepared, out of ideas, hungry, and scared. We're darn lucky we aren't in that situation. We weren't prepared, either. We barely had enough to get by. It's lucky for us you had your ex-husband and his uncle."

"You've been incredible, Malcolm. No man could have done more. You held the block together and defended us when no one else could have," Ellie said vehemently.

"Don't worry, baby. I'm not beating myself up. I know Vince is good at this stuff. I'm okay with that. I still win, because I have you." He smiled and squeezed her leg. "All I'm saying is that it cost so little in terms of money and time to be prepared, and so few did it. It's like an insurance policy I wish I'd bought. Think about it: if there was no Vince or Dave Cavanaugh, how much longer would it have been before I would have done bad things to keep you and Kate safe and fed?"

"You wouldn't—" Ellie began before Malcolm cut her off.

"I would. I've already thought about it a lot. I would, and I don't regret it. I think I'm still a good man because I would do bad things to keep you two safe. I think a lot of Vince because he came for you two, but also because he saved me from me."

While Ellie and Malcolm knew the area well, now it was as if they didn't know it at all. They looked at each building differently, scanning for threats. They worried about who might be waiting to hurt them and what building could provide shelter if they needed to take cover in a hurry. It was a whole new world. At least they were making good time.

"I wasn't sure leaving Chicago was necessary," Ellie said, gazing out the window. "I went along because I trusted people. Deep down, I thought everyone might be overreacting. I thought things would settle down soon and that I just wasn't used to life in the big city."

"This isn't normal for Chicago, baby." He reached over to wipe a tear from her cheek.

"I know. It's just so much more overwhelming than I expected. You were right. We do need to leave here."

Ellie turned back to smile reassuringly at Kate, who was listening and taking it all in. It was a lot to process.

VINCE

While Junior drove, Vince was searching for a certain kind of spot.

Not far from Ellie's house, he located a tight alley strewn with weeds and garbage. The view back down to Ellie's block, as well as to the route that the others had taken down Cicero Avenue, was exactly what he was looking for.

"Junior, back into that alley. We want to be back far enough not to be noticed, just not so far back that it obstructs our vision. We need to see as far down to Ellie's house as possible while still having a good field of vision toward Cicero where the others went. The shadow of the alley should cover most of the truck if we're careful."

"Okay, it feels like we're setting up the truck like a sniper's nest."

"That's right," Vince said. "It's only in the movies that the sniper hangs his rifle out a window or over a ledge. Anyway, nudge me when you see something." Vince reclined his seat and tipped his hat forward to shade his eyes.

Junior's jaw dropped in amazement. "How can you sleep right now?"

Vince smiled. "You were a soldier. Liz said you're a Marine. Is that right?"

"Yeah. At least you called me a Marine. Civilians keep saying 'former' Marine."

"Don't get too full of yourself, jarhead," Vince teased. "Anyway, didn't you ever learn to sleep whenever you could get it? That's a universal thing all soldiers in all armies learn fast."

"Yeah, but we were just in a firefight. Now here we are setting up as bait for another."

"That's all true. We have a few minutes before they come out, *if* they do," Vince said calmly. "It could be a while before they show."

"Okay," Junior said, shaking his head at Vince.

"Besides, I need the rest. Resting my eyes before a fight is my own Zen breathing exercise. If I can relax my mind and breathing, then I can be rested and calmer than my opponent when the fight comes. Hopefully, that calm and focus will help me make better decisions and more deliberate shots." Junior wasn't sure if he should be impressed or if Vince was poking fun at him. He just smiled and said, "Okay, man, I'll wake you."

LIZ

Liz opted to ride with Andy and Dwight. She wanted to get to know these men. Besides, the other two vehicles were crowded with people and supplies. Andy smiled and was friendly when he spoke. Dwight was more withdrawn. Neither man encouraged the small talk; they kept scanning all around the vehicle. Liz contented herself to sit back and try to help keep an eye out as well. She still carried the pistol that she hadn't fired. With these two men, she doubted she would need to.

She tried listening to the radio communications. Both Andy and Dwight took turns using the push-to-talk button in random patterns. Those moments of pushing the button interspaced by long moments of silence finally got on her nerves.

"What is all that about?" she asked. "Why do you keep pushing the button and saying nothing? Are you two as nervous as I am?"

Surprisingly, it was Dwight who responded. "We are nervous, ma'am. Maybe not like you, though. This is our business, so it's like you being live on stage in front of a lot of people. I'm sure you feel a rush of nervous energy or butterflies, but it's not debilitating. You know what you need to do. It's the same for us on a mission."

"I guess I understand that. It's just hard to comprehend it all right now." Liz sighed. "Why all the button pushing and not saying anything? It's driving me crazy. I don't know what's going on."

"That's exactly it, ma'am," said Andy. "If anyone else is listening, they don't know, either. For anyone listening to this frequency on the walkie talkie, all they can hear is a slight difference or interruption in the static for a moment. Those changes are like Morse code to one of us on the other end. We have a short set of pre-arranged signals that we all know what it means. That way we know what's going on and any bad guys won't."

"So what *is* going on?!"

"Nothing," Dwight answered, deadpan.

"Nothing? All that clicking for nothing?" Liz said in exasperation.

"Welcome to the way of war, ma'am." Andy grinned. "It's a few moments of stark terror interspaced with a whole lot of nothing."

"Uggh," Liz said. She leaned back in her seat, looking more like a teenage girl than a world-renowned star.

"If you're not very careful during these periods of nothing," Dwight cautioned, "then the next moment of stark terror could be the death of you or someone you care about."

"That's pretty depressing, don't you think?" Liz said. "I don't want to be on either end."

"Like we said, that's the way of war and the world, ma'am." Dwight spoke with a soldier's philosophy. "That's why most people try to avoid war. Most people should never be exposed to it. It's scary to think that people will kill each other and try to exterminate whole nations for something that most participants don't even understand."

"Why do it then?" Liz asked, recalling some of the anti-war and anti-violence demonstrations she'd seen in Los Angeles.

"If you're truly asking me *why* as a quest for knowledge," Dwight said, "and not a rhetorical *why* that comes from the left, I'll tell you."

"I want to know what you think," Liz said, avoiding the sarcasm.

"Well, some wars are stupid and shouldn't be fought. Some have to be fought because it's the price of freedom and a way of life. Too many people trade peace for a little oppression or a few freedoms lost. The problem is that oppressors and tyrants can never be fulfilled. They always want more. Sometimes, by the time you fight back, it's too late and the cost in lives is too high. Had the problem been dealt with early on, it could have been done cheaper and with less loss of life."

"So what about all this?" Liz asked. "Who is the tyrant here?"

"We are," Dwight replied. "All tyrants are not a single person. Real life doesn't always have a terrible villain that wears a black hat. We've created a massive and hungry central government that needs to be fed. It's like a drug abuser; it's so addicted to money and power, it's reached a level where it must lie, cheat, and steal to feed its habit. It has a whole subculture of people tricked into serving its habit like a codependent who needs Al-Anon. The people who expect the government to be their big brother, mentor, and provider do so because it's so ingrained in their ideology. They feed it and grow it so that in turn it will think for them and feed and provide for them. It reminds me of some of those people that raise a tiger cub in suburbia. It's cute when it's small."

"A smart man told me that the founding fathers once warned that our form of government could only work as long as the majority of the people were moral and lived an ethical Christian-based life in service to country and not the other way around. Is that close to what you're saying?" Liz asked.

"That's the root of it," Dwight answered. "People have changed and created this huge, unethical, hungry being in the central government that's crying to be fed. It in turn feeds its tenders. It's now too big to be fed. There are too many tenders and not enough providers. The bastions of morality that it takes to make this type of government work have eroded beyond a critical mass. The system is tearing itself apart. Those tenders who make excuses and feed this huge system don't know how to feed themselves, so they riot when things don't work the way they expect or someone isn't there to hand them food, checks, and promises. That's why we have this chaos going on."

Liz merely nodded. This was an overwhelming change to the life she was living only a few weeks ago. What was scary was that it had a ring of truth. "So what about people like me who don't want to be a victim and don't want to kill? I understand what you're saying about the takers. I don't want to be that, either. What do people like me do?"

"You do what you've always done. You find a wall manned by good people to hide behind," Dwight said.

"What do you mean hide behind a wall?" Liz said indignantly. "I've been out there among the people my whole life."

Dwight glanced back at Liz before responding, wanting to gauge her reaction. "The wall isn't always a physical wall. Sometimes it's another type of protection. Make no mistake, though. People in America, and especially the wealthy and pretty ones, can't live the way they do without protection. The wall is at the edge of our country and the extent of our power as a people and the limit of our faith and power as a country. People don't understand or appreciate that people like me, Andy, and Vince were manning that wall many miles away. Sometimes it's the police in your city or the powers of our laws that provide protection; nevertheless, it's there in some form. It's all of that that allows people to go to work or the store and have their social media and make their movies and a million other things they value."

"Okay, but what's changed? Why is it ending now?" Liz countered.

Dwight took a breath, trying to decide how to best describe what he wanted to say. "Because that wall around the country or at the extent of our power as a nation is a very long and expensive wall in practical terms. What is more is that it's a moral wall that wraps us in the cocoon of our belief system. Both of those need support from home. When finances are strained and morals weaken, the people manning the wall weaken as well. There are fewer people protecting us and fewer pastors keeping the country proud and morally upstanding so that we value virtue. Without strength and virtue, this country cannot stand."

"Is it all just chaos now? Do we live like Mad Max?" Liz asked with a hint of anger in her voice.

"That's possible, although I doubt we're quite there yet," Dwight countered with a hint of gallows humor in his voice. "There is still meat on this carcass to be picked at, and we are too huge to go down with the first punch. We are running out of gas, though. The virtuous people and the ones willing to man both that spiritual and physical wall when they are being attacked from behind as well as in front are growing fewer and fewer."

"So what now? We just go hide in a cabin somewhere?"

"Kind of," Dwight said as if he were teaching now. "The value of a community has always been in the combined efforts of those who are part of it. A single man can defend himself and possibly his family. A clan can defend a few dozen or a hundred people at most. A village or community can defend much more. A confederation or nation can defend so much more again.

"A single man, family, or clan expends all its efforts just to keep the family safe and fed. When your defenses are strong on a scale that only a community can support, then you have the luxury to focus on art, science, religion, education, and those types of things. We in this country have long forgotten those are luxuries and not rights."

"I think I get what you're saying," Liz said.

"At whatever level you can have a common goal or belief system, you can have a strong defense and eventually a safe place to grow and develop all those other things I just mentioned," Dwight said. "In the Army, a squad can defend each other because we're all on the same page. As a single family, you often have a common belief, and that's easy to align on. However, you spend most of your time defending and none on building. At a clan level, you can still have a pretty common belief system, and just a few people can be spared for education, religion, or art. At a village level, you can go further and create charity and deeper religion or art or education. At a national level, you stand on the shoulders of giants and can create huge advances in art, education, learning, and so forth. Nations live and die in the course of history because in our pursuit of advancements and leisure we always lose the virtue that got us there. That begins the rot from within. It takes decades and sometimes centuries to die. But die it does, then another nation is born to take its place."

"That sounds pretty much like what I've heard before by the same man who told me about things our founding fathers planned for. He talked about how this nation would fail when people lost their moral compass and their Christian-based dedication to service and doing something for a higher and better cause," Liz said.

"By the way," Dwight asked, "who told you all that?"

"Vince's uncle. Dave Cavanaugh."

Andy and Dave nodded in unison, "Makes sense."

"So what's going on with the radios?" Liz asked, changing the topic.

Andy and Dwight continued scanning the area around them while they spoke. "Not much, actually," Andy answered. "We decided beforehand that a couple of push to talk clicks on the button means I'm checking in and all is clear. Three is an acknowledgement that I heard and I'm okay, all is going according to plan. In that case, Vince doesn't need to know where I'm going or anything that I'd have to put in words for others to hear. He just needs to know I'm all right and the plan is still good and vice versa. If something hot is going on and we need to talk, we'll hold down the push to talk button for a moment and talk in fragments or code we understand so anyone listening in won't know what's going on or who is broadcasting. Speaking in the clear on these handhelds units is a last resort."

It wasn't long before a different series of radio breaks followed what was obviously a locked open *push to talk* button. She could hear Vince whisper to Junior to stay in the truck and be ready to get going fast. Then she heard a door open and someone get out, followed by what sounded like a huge amount of gunfire and an explosion, then more gunfire. Pretty soon an engine in the distance raced for a moment and then it shut down. More gunfire, and a few moments later the car door shut and two clicks on the push to talk. Andy responded with three clicks before setting down the walkie talkie with a chuckle.

He kept on driving as he muttered under his breath, "Yeah, he's hard to kill."

———

It was getting dark when Andy maneuvered the SUV through a cluster of industrial buildings to a nondescript building away from the others. The building appeared as if it hadn't gotten much use even before the recent chaos. Andy stopped in front of a large industrial overhead door, opened it, and ushered them all inside, and closed the door behind them. He and Dwight set up a watch schedule for the observation spots. After that was done, Andy unloaded some supplies and called for volunteers to help get some food ready. For now, they would be either eating cold food or something that could be warmed on Sterno cans.

"Why can't we have a larger fire?" Carol asked. "We're cold, hungry, and scared. A fire would help a lot."

Liz was happy that Carol was coming back around. She'd been so shell-shocked after Jennifer's death, the horrors they witnessed at the Waldorf, and the trek through Chicago. Liz was worried about her.

"In the dark, a fire can be seen through cracks and windows very easily," Andy said. "The smell of food travels even farther than the glow of a flame under certain conditions. We're still in danger. We just made it out of the worst part of Chicago safely. Let's not push our luck."

"Okay," Carol said. Liz was glad she didn't push it.

When Liz got a moment to talk to Andy away from the others, she wanted to unload a bit and get his reactions. "I can't believe we made it all the way down Cicero and out of the city. I suppose this is old hat to you soldiers."

Andy chuckled. "None of this is old hat. We've all fought overseas. Those cities were tiny compared to Chicago, and we had clear rules of engagement. I'm not saying it was easy. It wasn't. This is home, though. It's our country. We don't know who's a threat and who isn't, and that's a stressor that makes this much harder."

"I never thought of it that way."

"Most people don't. We're trained to kill, and we totally understand that power. It's a heavy burden to carry. People like Vince and Dwight carry it a lot heavier than people like me. Although it weighs on all of us."

"I guess I understand," Liz said, still somewhat confused.

Andy paused a moment to gather his thoughts. "We passed a dozen ambush sites today as we headed south. Every time we did, you got a little bit scared because you're just starting to learn about combat. You were watching for people hiding with guns and evil intentions. You wondered who was a threat and where it was coming from. Am I right?"

"Yes."

"That's good. Keeping your head on a swivel and identifying threats is a good way to stay alive long enough to learn more. Dwight, Vince, and me all know we can survive through most of the worst of this. The rest of you and the bad guys aren't trained like we are. Of course, there is always the possibility of a bullet with our name on it, an event we couldn't plan for or dodge, or an overwhelming force. We don't spend a lot of time thinking about that because soldiers get used to living with that early in their combat careers. It sucks, yet it's a constant buzz deep in our consciousness that just *is*."

Liz nodded, understanding dawning.

"What gets a lot of men like Vince and Dwight is the awesome power and responsibility that comes with looking at those people we pass and wondering if today we'll kill some of them. No matter how correct our choice or righteous our cause, we still know we could be taking away a husband, a father, or a provider. Did we judge properly? Did we need to kill? That's a heavy load to live with."

"I get it," Liz said.

"Not totally you don't. The thoughts I just shared are the deadliest thoughts a soldier can have for him and his buddies. So when a soldier stops to think and not react, he's lost his edge. He gets killed and gets a buddy or two killed with him. So we react, and later when things calm down, we pray we chose well. Then we live with what kind of man we are for killing without pause."

"Wow!"

"It's easy to kill when you know for sure your life or your friend's life is in danger. By the time you know for sure you need to kill, it's usually too late. It's instinct to kill quickly before it can be done to you, a split-second decision to choose when to unleash the dogs of war and when to run or negotiate.

"I observed around a hundred people as we passed today. I had those thoughts. Who might I need to kill? Who wasn't actually bad but was desperate to feed a sick or hungry child? Maybe I've lost my edge. A lot of soldiers do at some point in their career. I'll have to see tomorrow or the next day. Hopefully my brain didn't feel the threat was imminent and allowed my mind to wander. You can't know what it feels like on the inside to see all those people we've passed mile after mile and live with the weight of what I might have to do and then live with the guilt of having those thoughts because I might get a buddy killed by having them and hesitating. Every chokepoint or potential ambush spot we went through, I feared for them as much as for us. I kept praying, '*Please God, just let us through. Put fear in their hearts so they choose an easier target.*'" Andy took a shaky breath.

"That's scary," Liz said. It was odd for her to hear the normally playful Andy be so serious.

Then Andy let out a huge smile. "And here we are safe and sound, hidden away with food and friends! See? It's all about small victories."

"Well, Dwight doesn't seem too happy, and Vince isn't here yet."

"Dwight carries the weight of some hard stuff with him. None of us truly know what all he's seen and done. He signed up for this gig to get back home and protect people. I think he hopes all this will redeem him somehow. He doesn't talk about it much."

"What about Vince?" Liz queried.

"Vince is worse. He thinks he can control everything because he's so good and has had so much success. That's the worst kind of delusion. No one can talk him out of it, though," Andy said soberly.

"Why talk him out of it?"

"Because if you think you can control it all, then every person you kill, every soldier that doesn't make it home, becomes your fault. I trust Vince with my life. People tell stories about how good he is, but no man is perfect. He carries the weight of every person he's killed, every mission that wasn't perfect, and every solider that didn't come home like an anvil around his neck. He doesn't focus on all the people that lived because of the good choices he made. He needs to think about how many more would have died if someone else had led. If he doesn't get over that, it will cripple him emotionally. I hear it came close a few years back."

"What about Ellie and Kate? Can't they help?" Liz asked.

"I wasn't around him then, but men talk. He was just too involved in his own issues to let them help back then. He's a little better now. A woman has to have a life too, though. Ellie needed to move on, and she did. She gets him, and I think a part of her feels disloyal for moving on. Deep down, Vince understands and knows she did the right thing. That still doesn't make it easier."

Part Twenty-One

RESPITE

"*We sleep safely at night because rough men stand ready to visit violence on those who would harm us.*"

- Winston S. Churchill

VINCE

Vince had mapped out the safest route back to Peotone.

The rest should have already made it there. Miraculously, no one reported any need to fight heading south on Cicero. It was like an angel riding on their shoulders considering all the damage and crime they passed. Now wasn't the time to let down their guard. Peotone had seen violence too, and there were bad people and hungry people everywhere. Vince was driving, and he'd asked Junior to ride shotgun. It wasn't that he didn't trust Junior; it was that he hadn't worked with him before. Blacking out the headlights to a small slit was dangerous. While you could see directly in front of you, peripheral vision was severely limited. Vince was more experienced and confident in his skills to drive under those conditions.

As they approached Peotone, Vince hoped they were past the worst of things. When he began seeing fields, barns, and less destruction, he let out a breath he didn't know he'd been holding. They covered the last few miles to the warehouse in the dark with only the slits of blackout lights. The building was near where they stayed on the way up, and there didn't appear to be anyone else around. His first choice would have been to keep the group going until noon that day, then try to find a building that hadn't been used for a while with a good field of view. But they were tired and had made good time getting out of Chicago and needed a chance to regroup. Dwight, Andy, and the main group were already at the warehouse waiting for him and Junior.

Vince liked the building Dwight chose; his instincts were solid. The building was a weed-covered cinderblock building with a metal roof and glass windows that had been painted black many years ago. The roof sagged some, and Vince didn't know how Dwight was sure he could open the doors without a chain and a tow truck. It sat back off the road among a large industrial compound that didn't appear as if it had been used in years. He gave it a cursory onceover as he approached and mentally planned to do a more detailed scout after they were settled in. Although Dwight could have done the scout, that was the kind of thing he preferred to do himself. It settled his mind.

The Dollar General store near the warehouse was now not only looted but burned out as well. The good news was that there didn't appear to be anyone near it and not many places left to hide.

Vince picked up the walkie talkie. "Give me two flashes of light and open the door."

"Roger," Dwight responded.

When he got inside, he liked the ability to get deeper in the building and position the vehicles in a way to help conceal light or sound. Vince got his SUV parked in the warehouse, and everyone gathered to ask questions. He spoke to the group while focusing directly on Andy and Dwight. "I want to scout a bit and make sure I wasn't followed and no one saw your light."

The civilians didn't understand why he wanted to go back out. Junior and Andy nodded. Dwight merely gave another, "Roger."

"I know it's not easy, but you all need to try and get some sleep," Vince said to the group. "We need to be back on the road between two and three in the morning. It comes fast. You all need your rest."

"Vince, two AM is early. It feels safe here. We're all tired and stressed out. Can't we get a few more hours' rest?" Liz said.

Vince shook his head before she even finished speaking. "We're still too close to Chicago. This safety is an illusion. If hoodlums find this warehouse, we're boxed in. This can be a trap as much as a haven."

"Okay," she replied, her voice betraying her weariness.

"Besides, it's like I said before, we have our safest period of travel between about three AM and noon tomorrow. That's when the thugs are sleeping off the previous night's binge. They're lazy in general, and that's the best time for us to be on the move. We need to make the most of it."

Malcolm nodded. "I agree."

"Keep this in mind," Vince cautioned, "while Andy, Dwight, Junior, and I can fight, I have you all to think about. For now, I'd rather run than fight, because in a fight anything can go wrong."

It wasn't lost on Vince that the body language of others in the group improved when Malcolm agreed with him. Malcolm had natural leadership, and people responded well to him. That might come in handy down the road.

Vince slid out into the darkness on foot through a small side door to surveil the avenues of approach from the shadows and see if they were followed. He was at home in the dark. It was a place to let his mind find a peaceful spot and be in control of his circumstances. The darkness covered him like a blanket. He stayed close to the building and let his mind almost subconsciously sift through the sounds of the night, wind blowing across loose tin roofing, critters digging through garbage, cats fighting in the distance. They were all normal sounds and allowed Vince's mind to relax. Had there been some movement, sound, or shadow that didn't fit in with what was natural for this place, he would have been on instant alert. It had been a stressful day, and this was a good way for him to relax and take stock of the day and himself, alone and in the dark.

LIZ

Most of the people around Liz were trying to relax.

There were pallets of blankets and people in different states of rest. The concrete floor had a thick layer of dirt and dust, leaving most people to find a spot in the cars or on a table or work bench. It was easy to tell there was very little sleeping going on. As tired as everyone was, they were filled with bundles of nervous energy, most of all Dwight. He was like a caged cat, silently pacing from window to door and back in the warehouse. Andy was just the opposite. As soon as he lay down, he was sound asleep, which Liz confirmed by the rhythmic rising and falling of his chest.

She was sitting next to Junior on a wooden pallet covered by cardboard and blankets, her back against a car. Both were tired, yet neither could sleep. "What happened back there when you and Vince stayed behind?" she asked quietly. "We heard shots and an explosion. It was hard to tell if all the shooting was from you two or what was going on."

"Oh, man," Junior said with an expression that was an odd mixture of awe and weary acceptance. "Vince is the real deal. It was spooky how calm he was. I've seen Special Forces men in my career and some very good ones. I've seen men who may have been stronger or better in hand to hand combat. I don't think I've ever seen that level of dead calm and drive toward a mission in a man's eyes, though."

Junior glanced over at Liz's face to see if she was getting it. It was hard to describe an emotion, especially like Junior experienced when seeing Vince in action. "He actually set a trap for those thugs...only me and him against them. He had no idea how many there would be. It was like we had them outnumbered, not the other way around. We needed to stop them or else. He planned it and didn't show any doubts at all. I don't think he needed me or even cared I was there."

"I'm sure you were a much bigger help than you admit. I know men don't say thanks well," Liz said supportively.

Junior shook his head. "Then, of all things, he took a nap! He took a freaking *nap*! I asked him how he could sleep at a time like this. I thought he was merely getting comfortable. I didn't believe he could actually sleep."

"What did he say?" Liz asked.

"He said it was his Zen mindset," Junior answered incredulously. "He said he used mental downtime to relax and get into a calm state before the killing."

"What happened after that?"

"Sure, as shit...pardon me, ma'am, but sure as shit he wasn't asleep for fifteen minutes when two carloads of gang members met in front of Ellie's house and got themselves all riled up. Even though I couldn't hear what they were saying, it was easy to see they were howling mad and pointing at the house and bodies and yelling. A couple of them even shot in the air a couple times."

"What did Vince do?"

"He cocked one eye open and said they'll be headed our way in a while, that they needed to get themselves a bit more psyched up first. Then he closed his eyes again and went back to sleep."

Liz was almost speechless. "That was it?"

"Yeah, then they got in the cars and headed our way on the trail you all took. At the moment they loaded up and headed after you all, he stepped out of the truck and knelt behind a low concrete wall off to our left. He told me to sit tight and be ready. The first car came into the kill zone Vince had marked with some bottles and other debris. He shot into the driver's side window, then the tires and engine, making the car swerve to the left and onto a curb, then he rattled off a volley of shots into the cab at the men. He likes to carry that sweet Winchester SX-AR .308 semi auto. I know you don't know guns, ma'am, but that's pretty much the same as the FN .308 that's respected around the world. His has the heavy barrel which makes it more accurate for long-range shots. Those .308 rounds can sure do some damage.

"I don't know how many men were inside the car to start or hurt or dead after his barrage. It was something like six or seven men that came up firing between the two cars when he paused. Vince stepped back behind the concrete barrier as casually as you please to reload, like it was part of the plan."

Liz was hanging on his every word. "What did you do?"

"I didn't know if he wanted me out there throwing lead or if he wanted me in the truck and ready to drive. When the hoodlums returned fire, I thought Vince was pinned down. I was about to open up and help him even though he told me to sit tight. Then he turned to me and the guy was smiling. He had a freaking smile on his face! It's like they were all following the script in his play.

"He held up a hand to me in a motion to stay where I was. Then he pulled out a hand grenade and tossed it between the two cars, right at the gangsters. It tore them up. Everyone on that block was shell-shocked except for Vince."

"Is that when you two left to catch up to us?"

"No. That's when he stood up and walked in on them liked he was shooting skeet. He never hurried, and every time one poked his head up, Vince shot them. When he got close, there were two left behind the last car randomly firing rounds over the door. Vince put three rounds through the door where a man was taking cover. He fell, and the gun skidded away and the blood pooled. It was obvious he was done. Vince wasn't taking chances, though. He stayed at an angle that would be tough for them to get a shot at him without exposing themselves and skipped a couple of rounds under the car. When the last man moved behind a tire, Vince stepped sideways around the car in a quick pie move and killed him."

"Oh my God."

"Vince pulled his handgun and methodically put down the rest with headshots. I know it sounds harsh, but it's understandable if you knew what they planned for us and you ladies. We can't take a chance on anyone like that following us."

Junior noticed the sickly expression on Liz's face and regretted sharing so much detail.

"I'm not sure I agree we needed to execute them."

"Ma'am, you might be right, but I was beyond questioning him by that time. He got in the second car and drove it beside the first to block the road then got out and shot into the engine and tires with his rifle to disable it."

"Why block the road? Did he think there were more? Couldn't they take another route?"

"I don't know," Junior said. "It would definitely slow them down if there were more. Vince got in the SUV, keyed the mike twice, and asked me to drive. He said it all so calm and polite like I was taking him to the store or something. Man, that dude is cold."

"Couldn't he have gotten shot walking right up on them like that? That doesn't sound smart."

"Yeah. Everything I've been taught says that's foolhardy. While it might work a time or two, eventually the odds will catch up and you'll end up shot. I asked him about that later on our way here."

"What did he say?"

"That's just it. I see why men follow him. He said he needed to kill them, that it was his family and innocent people like you we're protecting, and that he didn't want to imagine what they had planned for the rest of the group if we didn't stop them. He said he would take a bullet to keep you women safe."

Junior peered into Liz's eyes. "It wasn't a suicide mission. He did weigh the risks and decided to walk right into them. He said that since he and I had never worked together, he didn't want to guess what I'd be doing in a firefight, and because my primary mission is to take care of you, he didn't want me in the middle of that fight unless he absolutely needed to."

"It still sounds risky to me. Anything could have gone wrong."

"Yes, that's true, and he could probably tell I still had my doubts because he elaborated to say we had one chance when they were totally confused to take them out. After he hit the first vehicle hard and blocked the road, they'd be raging mad and not thinking straight. That was his chance to even the odds with a grenade. They would never be expecting that. Vince admitted it was harsh, but it's a war to save his family."

"Okay, but did he need to kill them?"

"I asked him that. I mean, as bad as things are, it's still America. He said it's possible he went too far; it's a choice he chose to make on a split second and something he'd have to live with. He didn't want me to have to live with that choice, too. He explained that at that moment he was thinking how hard it would be to keep our group safe if any of them told other gang members where we were headed. With all that in mind, he chose to put the scum down rather than to leave them to hurt anyone else."

"Does that mean we're safe?"

"No, there will be other gangs and threats. He pointed out that I may not have seen his last rifle shot down the street before switching to the handgun. There was another car back down the block that was laying back. He put a round through the windshield before they were able to back around a corner. It was a long way off, so he couldn't be sure, although the gangster in the passenger seat resembled the one with the huge scar and the lazy eye from back on Ellie and Malcolm's block. I asked him if he thinks they could be coming after us, and he said we're probably okay. They're nothing more than local gangbangers. We're getting the hell out of dodge. That gang lost a lot of their men and transportation. There's more low-hanging fruit here in this area. It wouldn't make any sense to follow us."

Liz was a bit rattled. "I'll admit I'm clearly out of my element, Junior. Thank you for everything."

After a few minutes of silence, Junior added one more thing. "When we were riding down the road, Vince told me it was Aristotle who said, '*We make war that we may live in peace.'* Then he just went back to scanning his side of the road and didn't say anything else. He's an odd dude."

———

Liz's conversation with Junior made her mind race and wouldn't let her sleep, although her body was more tired than she could remember. Andy and Dwight insisted they couldn't have a fire and could only heat food with Sterno cans.

Staying hypervigilant was exhausting, and the stress didn't help much. During the meal, she was relieved the men said they would be sleeping until about two in the morning. The thought of sleeping for several hours sounded like heaven after the last few days, even though her mind probably wouldn't allow it. While the men divided up guard duty, Liz resigned herself to a restless night with a racing mind. She decided she might as well get comfortable and accept it.

"Ma'am, it's time to get up." Junior shook her gently. "We need to get back on the road."

"We just got here." Liz stretched her neck to work out the kinks. "Is something wrong? Have we been found?" she asked in alarm as her mind shed the cobwebs of sleep.

"No, you've been out for about five hours."

It was then that Liz noticed someone had covered her with a blanket and put another rolled-up one under her head. "Thanks for this, Junior," she said

"It wasn't me," Junior said. "Vince did it. I'm not sure how he didn't wake you."

"I thought we were supposed to share a turn on guard. Why didn't anyone wake me?"

"Vince told us to let you sleep. He said the same for Ellie and Kate, although Ellie was up all night."

"What about Carol?"

"She slept like the dead as soon as we got here, then woke around midnight. Vince didn't want her near the door, so he assigned her to watch the supplies and vehicles."

"I feel bad for her, but I suppose that's for the best," Liz said.

Liz reflected that she should have been insulted that they skipped her, although she was too tired and worried about Carol to care much at the moment.

LEVI

Levi got everything loaded into Greg's truck.

Thankfully Greg brought some cargo straps to ratchet down the cases from the plane. When they finished loading, Levi saw the captain paying for the fuel. The Springfield airport manager made himself a little more money by selling the crew a few sandwiches for silver coins.

While the rest of the world was in meltdown mode, Greg was happy, joking, and just as unconcerned as when things were normal. Greg's wife Camille, Cami, was a bubbly and happy person much the same as Greg. She sat in the back seat of the truck with a smile on her face and a small dog in her lap.

Levi offered to get in the back, but Cami would have none of it. "No, you two need to talk. Greg and I talk all the time."

"Okay," Levi said, still uncomfortable sitting up front while Cami sat in the back.

"Besides," Greg said, "if we have trouble, you can sit up front and scare the scalawags off."

"Are you expecting trouble?" Levi asked, his defenses suddenly on alert.

"Heck no, I didn't want you to get bored. You soldier types always need someone to fight or protect."

"How can you be so sure you won't have trouble?" Levi asked.

"Because the only two kinds making trouble are the city slickers and the redneck riffraff we already have. I don't expect us to run into either of those. The city types are usually afraid of the country. Coming out here scares them more than robbing each other in town. They aren't hungry enough yet to overcome that fear."

"What about the local rednecks?"

"We all know who they are. They're all living on the dole. This chaos is worse for them than us. They don't get stuff for free, and they aren't protected by the law right now if they get caught with their hands in the wrong cookie jar. That doesn't mean they won't try. It means they probably won't do it head on during the daylight. They'll try to steal behind our backs while we sleep."

"It sounds like you're confident in your neighbors and their ability to remain safe."

"I trust in the Lord," Greg said. "There aren't enough of us, though. When a bad guy dies, three more pop up. When a good man dies, we're all diminished. When a man sees his child go hungry, he may do bad things. When a good man is forced to do bad things, that's the same as a good man dying."

"So what can we do?" Levi asked.

"Trust in the Lord. Our church is running missions to check on our members and a few other local people. We're keeping each other fed and in some cases moving families in together. If this goes on longer, we'll have to make better plans."

"Where is the food coming from? Did you all have stored food in preparation?"

"Some of us did. Not nearly enough, though. Yesterday we butchered one of my cows and brought the meat around to several families. Everyone had to cook it right away. That bought us a couple days."

"That sounds good. Will driving me to Carrolton take you away from the church and your mission to serve your neighbors?"

"No, there are other men. Plus, Cami and I need a break. We want to go to that restaurant and see how things are going. We're worried about Vince too."

"He's like family to us," Cami said from the back.

After a mile or so of silence, Greg said to Levi, "Is there a chance you have accepted Christ as your savior?"

Levi chortled deep in his chest. "No, I'm Jewish. My parents would die if they even knew I was having this conversation."

"Sorry, I didn't mean to pry. It's that with all that's going on, I worry. I do wonder what God thinks. Some people think we're in a very critical biblical time right now."

"I can see where they might think that," Levi responded diplomatically.

"Any chance you're a messianic Jew?" Greg asked.

"No, although I have to admit they have a very interesting belief that I'd be more inclined to listen to if it weren't for my family and how it would kill them."

This time Greg nodded with mirth in his eyes. "I'll let it drop for now. Let's get you to Carrollton."

Part Twenty-Two

HEADING SOUTH

"When you have completed ninety-five percent of your journey, you are only halfway there."

- Japanese Proverb

Peotone, IL

Judith Patterson lay on the floor, her bloodied cheek resting on the tile, her gaze locked on her husband's lifeless eyes. The man with the scar cackled as he kept kicking both of them. Judith was past feeling rage; the torment lasted so long, time lost meaning. She was helpless and tired and in such terrible pain. She didn't fear death now. A world like this without her husband was not a place she wanted to be. The cold numbness in her body made her confident the Lord would grant her one last wish soon. She could feel during the beating the moment when something broke loose inside her. She lost consciousness on the floor of her kitchen and never expected to awake. She wished she hadn't. She was face to face with Larry, and his eyes were open, glazed over in death, and Judith couldn't move. She could only feel the cold floor on her cheek and the internal bleeding expanding in her stomach.

Judith and Larry were both in their late seventies. They had been high school sweethearts and lived in Peotone their entire lives with the exception of the four hardest years of Judith's life when Larry was in the Navy during Vietnam. It always hurt Judith that she couldn't have children. Larry never minded. They led an idyllic, charmed life and were enjoying their twilight years.

Even the loss of power and order hadn't been too bad. They had a generator, and Larry made sure they were stocked up on food and had several weeks' worth of their medicine. They spent their days reading, tending flowers, and enjoying each other.

That ended when the scar-faced man banged on their door.

"Go away!" Larry yelled through the door. "We don't have anything for you. There's nothing worth taking. I'm calling the cops."

The men kicked in the door. Larry offered them whatever they wanted, and most of the gang accepted that. They practically danced with excitement when they found the trove of pill bottles meant to last him and his wife through the crisis. For a brief moment, Judith hoped that they might only rob them and leave. Then the scar-faced man got a sadistic smile on his face and started kicking and beating them for no reason. They'd already stolen everything of value. His men stood back in silence. No one came to Larry and Judith's aid.

As her organs bled out inside her body, Judith heard the gang's elation at the food and drugs they stole. She could see the leader drinking a bottle of Pappy Van Winkle Larry saved and scrimped for and was keeping for a special occasion. The last thing she heard before she lost consciousness for good was their plan to hit more houses in her neighborhood. She wished she could warn her friends that were retired and the young family down the street with kids, but it was too late.

ELLIE

The night passed restlessly for many of them. Despite that, most of the people managed to get at least some sleep. By two AM, Vince and the other men got the vehicles packed up and checked out. A couple of people were still dozing during the commotion, and Andy made sure everyone else was up and ready.

Vince and Dwight worked with Malcolm to make sure his vehicles were configured for a night run like Vince's. They took some fuses out and checked to make sure that the dome, taillights, and other non-essential lights wouldn't potentially give them away. They used duct tape to hide everything except for a strip of the headlights and brake lights. During a break in the preparations, Ellie asked Malcom what they were doing.

Malcolm said, "It makes total sense. I'm mad at myself for not thinking of it ahead of time."

"What do you mean?" Ellie asked.

"Like Vince mentioned earlier, the safest time to be on the move is early morning. We may drive into the late afternoon sometimes, but we definitely need to be on the road by three."

"I get that. Won't it be harder to see without the lights?" Ellie asked.

"Yeah, although all those lights make us much easier to be seen too. Light can be seen from a long way off in the dark. We're especially visible when we get further out in the country where we don't have buildings to block the light. We need to be moving in darkness with very little light and noise. Vince's men were telling me that doing this to the vehicles will make them hard to see unless people are up close or at the right angle. Andy said it was like the Brits did during World War II."

"Well anything that keeps us safe is good by me. Be careful you don't rear end the car in front of you because you can't see it," Ellie cautioned.

VINCE

By this time, everyone in the warehouse was up and preparing for the day's trek. They would begin by traveling through the early morning darkness and then half the day or more. Vince made his rounds talking to each person. He looked them in the eye as he spoke to let them understand he was there if they needed him. His presence and demeanor calmed people. Vince strongly believed the most valuable thing you could give someone was your undivided attention, even if only for a few moments. Vince made sure to push each person to eat even though many said they were too nervous. He even got a smile out of Carol as she ate a bite of food.

When they were ready to leave, Vince gathered them around.

"We're going to try and hit it hard today. I don't want anyone going so fast that we're foolhardy or make mistakes. We need to get to Kentucky safely. Along the way, I have a friend that will shelter and feed us in French Lick, Indiana. It's a little out of our way. However, I know for sure it's safe, and we can get cleaned up there and have hot food. It's going to be a long, hard day.

"It took us a couple of days heading north. It might be worse now. I was willing to take risks coming up with only Andy, Dwight, and me that I won't with the girls along."

Andy feigned indignance. "Hey, boss that hurts."

Vince grinned. "Besides, even though I don't think we're being followed, I can't be sure. I have a weird feeling about this so I want to go fast and get to safety."

"Boss, if you want me to stay back," Dwight offered, "you can be sure your back trail will be clean."

"I don't doubt it, Dwight. If the bad guys got away or took another route, you couldn't follow them on foot, though. I don't want to rob the civilians of the vehicle and support you and Andy provide. We'll move fast and make it hard on anyone who might be following."

"It's not that we don't trust you on this. It's that I'm curious why. What if we can't make it?" Liz asked. She didn't mean to be challenging; she just got this way when she was nervous.

"I know what we came through coming north. We have a safe place with supplies in French Lick, and we need that safe home base. If we can't make it, then we'll find another place like this," Vince answered patiently, "I'll find a way to keep you safe. However, I would prefer to get to our forward operating base as fast as possible."

"Forward what?" Liz asked.

When Vince laughed, Liz noticed how his face changed completely and the worry lines melted away. "I'm sorry, I get so into the mission I slip right into military lingo. A forward operating base is what we call our safe location or supply area that is as far into enemy territory as makes sense. It's the right distance between the charter town in Kentucky and Chicago so that we can safely support it from Kentucky and it us on the mission in return. When I say it out loud like that, it sounds a little overdramatic. I don't think Gus and his family would appreciate their home and business being referred to as a forward operating base in enemy territory."

"Gotcha," Liz said, and it was her turn to smile.

Vince turned serious. "I plan to head us back much the way we came, moving as fast as circumstances will allow," Vince said. "After that, we'll cut over to Madison and across the river to home, or at least your new home for now."

Liz and several others in the group murmured assent. The men nodded, and Ellie put her hand in Malcolm's. They had a plan, and it was time to get moving.

After checking to make sure the vehicle changes were complete and everything was loaded, Vince and the men got all the cars lined up at the garage door ready to go.

"I'll be running ahead and sending back info and route changes," Vince said. "If a vehicle breaks down, we need to quickly move stuff to the next vehicle and leave it behind. We don't even stop to change a tire," Vince announced to the security men. "I want the civilian vehicles to stay in the middle. I need you two," he pointed to Andy and Dwight, "to take the rear position. You have to stay close to them. I know we generally keep more spacing, but I want your firepower close if it's needed. I don't think we have to worry a lot about IEDs, claymores, grenades, or shoulder-fired missiles like you might have overseas, so bunching up should be okay."

"Roger that," Andy said. "I've got the wheel. Dwight will be riding shotgun."

"My plan is to move out a mile or two ahead of you all. I may not always be in sight. Malcolm, I need you and Ellie in the first vehicle behind me," Vince instructed.

"Okay," Malcolm said. It was clear there was some confusion in his voice. Ellie was standing close by, very intent on the conversation.

"Malcolm, because I'm ranging ahead, I need someone I trust behind me keeping this convoy on the route. I can't spare Andy and Dwight from the drag position, so you're it." Vince had a way of using a man's name and making him feel critical. That made men rise to the occasion more often than not.

"Gotcha," Malcolm answered. "But how will I know where to go if I lose sight of you?"

"You will lose sight of me a lot, because I'll be moving out a mile or more ahead. I may choose to check out some side roads and ambush spots. It's even possible that I could fall behind. You have the map we gave you with the route marked. When I talk on the walkie talkies, I'll relay only some very simple and vague instructions if a change is needed."

"What if I miss it or don't know what you mean?" Malcolm asked, worried.

"If you don't understand or think you've missed what I'm talking about, don't hesitate to say something short into the walkie talkie like 'say again' or 'transmission garbled.' I'll know you need more information and give it to you another way."

"I suppose I'll know when I hear it. Will Andy and Dwight be listening in too?" Malcolm asked.

"Yes, they'll be listening, and they'll signal if they think you're going the wrong way."

"That's good," Malcolm said, clearly relieved.

"Listen for me to say things like 'two blocks straight' or 'left on M for Madison.' I don't want to give instructions that someone else listening in could understand without some thought, so you won't hear me say 'go three miles on Highway 50 and turn left on Wisconsin Street.' That's too easy for someone to figure out quickly. By being cryptic and moving fast, we should be long gone before someone figures it out."

"Okay," Malcolm said, nodding and with understanding.

"One more thing," Vince said. "I won't give you much instruction when we decide to stop for a rest. I'll just catch up to you and flash my lights for you to follow. I don't want people knowing where we stop. That's when we're most vulnerable."

"Got it."

Vince turned to head to his truck when Dwight stopped him. "Boss, what say we all start at channel two on the walkies and every time you give an instruction, we move up a channel? These go up to eleven, so when we hit eleven we go back to two and start over."

Vince nodded. "I like it, but what happens if someone misses a channel hop and misses an instruction?"

"Easy." Dwight grinned. "When we hear your instruction, Malcolm will respond by holding the push to talk button twice. I'll hold it three times and when that happens we all go up a channel. If someone doesn't respond we go back a channel, say the word 'hop' and try again."

Vince turned to Malcolm. "Are you good with this? We can take any part out or change it to make you comfortable. The cargo you have is the sole reason we're here. Ellie, the same goes for you too. Anything you want changed, now is the time to say so."

"I'm good," Malcolm said. "Besides, Andy and Dwight will be behind us, always in sight."

"Same for me," Ellie said.

MALIK

The group exited the warehouse after taking shelter for the night, unaware they were being watched by a scar-faced man hidden near the burned-out rubble of the Dollar General store.

He and his lieutenant had kept a long way back from the group as they came out of Chicago. He wanted to attack but didn't want to take any more chances. Malik would do this on his terms. During the trek south, he lost the group several times and found them again.

Late last night, they lost them again yet were confident they had gone to ground in one of the warehouses. It would be suicide to go close to the buildings searching for them. He was sure that some of those men had military training.

It was dumb luck that he couldn't sleep and was scanning the buildings in the area while pacing and hoping for a break. Malik had never been able to sleep long or soundly since spending time in that institution as a kid. The screaming and yelling would stick in his mind for the rest of his life. His brother had gotten him out, and life was good until the men he was hunting killed Raheem.

The remnants of the gang had been looting and were sleeping it off at a small home near a car dealership a block away. His lieutenant stood next to him after being woken from a drunken reverie with the toe of Malik's boot.

"Should I get some of the others ready?" he asked. "We could run them down and take them out then head back to our home turf."

"No, let's follow them. When we get a chance, we can take the women and kill the men easy and slow." Malik sneered evilly. "The women will wish for that fate. They will pay for what they did to my brother."

LEVI

Levi sat in the front seat of the red four-door Ford pickup with Greg. He was amazed at how calm Greg was. The rest of the country was shaking itself apart, and Greg acted like he was out for a Sunday drive, making jokes and laughing at them. He did lament the fact that some of his favorite restaurants were now closed.

Cami piped into to say that for a thin man Greg loved eating. He loved all the various country roadside diners. Cami proclaimed that Greg was personally known at many of the country diners in a three-county radius. He could make friends anywhere.

"We'll work our way north on Highway 55," Greg announced. "Shelbyville is still a mess, so we'll go around it. I know some of the police in Shelbyville and most are trying to get things set right. Right now, it's more than they can handle."

Skipping around Shelbyville would take them through Simpsonville, Kentucky, where Greg's farm was. Because it was late in the day, he suggested they spend the night there and get an early start to Carrollton in the morning. Then they would take some back roads to pick up Highway 55 again north of Shelbyville, taking them through Eminence and New Castle, Kentucky. Levi expressed some concern about going through those towns. Greg was confident it would be fine. Aside from knowing most everyone, Greg was certain those towns were full of good, solid people.

Each town had a few families or areas that produced most of the crime. Before the current crisis the police, community, and legal system had their hands tied as to how to handle those people. With how things were going, those were the families that needed to hunker down, not the good people like in the big cities. No one would be investigating a police shooting or a citizen self-defense case too vigorously right now. The criminals in the country towns were aware of that, and the ones that weren't wouldn't matter much if the country didn't right itself before much longer.

"After that we'll bypass another town called Campbellsburg and head straight into Carrollton," Greg said

"Why bypass Campbellsburg if Eminence and New Castle are okay to go through?"

"Well, it's probably fine too, although they have some rougher banditos." Greg snorted, and it was hard to tell whether he was teasing or not. "My friend Jim with the Shelbyville police told me Eminence and New Castle are stable. The local police and some citizens have seen to that. Campbellsburg had a bit more crime before, and I don't have much information on that town. I know you need to get to Carrollton safe and sound, and I do want to keep Cami safe, so we'll work around Campbellsburg. Besides, the road I want to take kind of naturally bypasses most of Campbellsburg anyway. After that, we can come up on Carrollton from the side that your charter town is on and not even have to go through Carrollton itself."

Levi nodded. "Sounds good to me."

Then Greg got that mischievous glint in his eye again. "Besides, Vince would never forgive me if I brought his big ol' soldier to Carrollton all scratched up." Greg cracked up at his own joke.

Levi sat back to watch the scenery. This was beautiful country. If you didn't know the whole country was in disarray, you could never tell by what he was seeing. They passed other vehicles occasionally and people on tractors working the fields every once in a while.

Levi tried to imagine Vince's mission and where he would be now. When they arrived in Carrollton, he would have to decide if he should wait for word from Vince or if he could be more help going to Vince's forward operating base in French Lick. He wanted to help but was too experienced a campaigner to go rushing off with little information.

Part Twenty-Three

UNEXPECTED

"He will win who knows when to fight and when not to fight."

- Sun Tzu

VINCE

This was always the hardest part of a mission for Vince.

He wanted to be the one to deal with trouble whenever it popped up, although he couldn't be all places at once. During the planning stage, he always did everything he could to ensure he had all the bases covered. Experience and the old axiom that *no plan survived the first engagement with the enemy* taught him to be cautious and watch for risks. Despite all the preparation in the world, you could never be sure where the trouble might come from.

When the group hit open road south of Peotone, Vince picked up the phone and called Gus Lancaster at the junkyard.

"Hello?"

"Wow, I'm surprised I got through to you on the first call," Vince said.

"Have these things been hard to use?" Gus asked.

"Yeah, haven't you tried using the one we gave you?"

"Nah, most everyone I care about is here. I keep it charged with the fold-out solar thing you gave me. This is the first call I've gotten."

"Well, it's been hard to get calls through. We don't know why."

"Maybe it's because you're calling people at 3:30 in the morning," Gus said gruffly.

"You're right, I'm sorry about that, Gus. That's the second time I've been called out for being so caught up in the mission I forget I'm a civilian at home. I should have waited to call."

"Well, you got me now. What can I do ya for?"

"I wanted you to know my plan is to make it to your place tonight. If I need to be coming in fast, don't shoot us. We have four vehicles."

"We've got you covered. Keep in touch if you need some help close to here. We can't go too far, though. I won't leave this place and my family undefended."

"Roger that."

───────

Sometime after sunrise, Vince came upon a roadblock and approached it cautiously. It was manned by local farm folk. He radioed back to the convoy to hold position while he checked it out.

Although the people were friendly, they still didn't want strangers coming through their area. They didn't allow Vince to get close and didn't want to talk much. He recognized they were just wary of strangers and tricks and only wanted to protect their community. They had probably already experienced some bad things and heard of more. After some haggling, one of the men on the roadblock came out and, with a map, suggesting an alternate route.

While they were talking, Vince couldn't shake the feeling they were being watched. He'd had that feeling since they left Chicago, and it was much stronger now than it had been this morning. He wanted to chalk it up to the probability that this community likely placed some hidden shooters in an overwatch position protecting their people on blockade duty. At the same time, Vince had learned to trust his intuition. It saved his life on more than one occasion. He didn't have time to scout too far for threats. They needed to keep moving.

From the man who came out to talk, Vince learned they were a farming community and had remained relatively intact during the chaos. They had a good supply of farm goods, feed, corn, and livestock. There was also a HAM operator in the community, and he got their call sign. He shared with him some basics about the Carrollton community and offered to have the HAM operator there reach out to them. Although this place was further than the Carrollton charter town needed for trading, you never knew what you might need or who might need you. It was always good to keep in touch with other communities trying to do things the right way.

It would require a bit of backtracking to go around their community, adding about two hours to their trip. It couldn't be helped. These people were only trying to defend their community, and it wouldn't be right to try and bust through only to save a couple hours' time.

The meeting was observed from a distance as well. Some of the gang that was left were tired of chasing this group and wanted to get this over and get back to their turf. They argued with Malik that they needed to attack the group or this community or something. They wanted women, guns, liquor, and food. What they found in Peotone wasn't enough. They were worried some of the other gangs in Chicago were getting fat while they were out in the country chasing these people. The world was a free for all now, and Chicago had all they needed. That wasn't what Malik wanted, though, and they feared him, so they followed his lead. He was as ruthless as his brother but crazy on a whole other level.

———

Some of the people in the convoy were a bit spooked when they got the command to find a secluded place to pull over. Andy and Dwight signaled to Malcolm and pulled in front to take the lead. Dwight found a dirt road to their right that went through some trees then disappeared into farm land. The weeds were grown up on the dirt road, and there was no mailbox. There was an old red rusted metal gate hanging open to the side.

Andy got on the walkie to Vince and said, "M46 off of 55, south dirt through trees."

When Vince responded with a simple, *"Roger,"* Andy keyed the push to talk button twice to let them know they were all on the same page.

Andy and Dwight circled the vehicles behind the trees, facing out toward the road. They instructed everyone to take the opportunity to relieve themselves and get something to eat and drink. Dwight worked with Junior and Malcolm to set up a guard.

"Watch the fields behind us from inside the tree line so you won't be seen," he instructed. "Blend in against a tree so you don't create a silhouette if anyone is watching. Andy, I want you next to the trucks and the women. I'll work back toward the road to see if anyone noticed us pulling off."

———

About twenty minutes passed when Dwight saw Vince's vehicle approaching the dirt road where they turned off. When Vince was close enough, Dwight stepped out onto the road. To anyone else watching, Dwight just melted away from the bush.

Vince lowered the window and waved to Dwight, who pointed toward the dirt road. Dwight scuffed up the tire tracks in the dirt with a tree branch after Vince pulled through, then pulled the old rusty gate hanging from a single hinge halfway across the path before following Vince back into the break area. When they got behind tree cover, Vince spoke to Dwight.

"I didn't plan on stopping, but it was a good chance to sweep our back trail. What did you see?"

"I saw a couple of cars pass earlier, but it's hard to tell if they were following or only using the same road."

Had Dwight been closer, he would have noticed that the two cars had Illinois license plates, and the men inside them wore matching colored bandanas on their arms.

"Okay, I guess that's good." Vince glanced apprehensively back at the road.

"You worried about something, boss?" Dwight asked.

"Nothing in particular. I can't put my finger on it, although a few times I've felt watched. If I could take the time, I'd find out for sure. If we are being followed, I could put us in more danger by leaving the group, though. If I slow us down to hunt our back trail, I may find trouble that wasn't there until we slowed down." Vince sighed in frustration.

"I hear ya. I've been looking over my shoulder a lot as well. But the goal is to get these people down the road. I didn't see an obvious threat, so I kept moving."

"Have you said anything to anyone?" Vince asked.

"No. I didn't want to scare anyone."

"What about Andy?"

"We haven't been alone where none of the others could hear, and it might be nothing. Besides, I'm usually on the perimeter, and it wasn't anything I could pin down," Dwight said, sounding exasperated.

"Me too."

"So why did we stop?" Dwight asked.

"I'll tell everyone at once," Vince answered. "It's not a big deal."

LIZ

Liz saw Vince heading back in to the shaded area behind the trees where they had pulled off, and she was both apprehensive and comforted that he was here.

The anxiety was about the change of plans, why they stopped, and wondering what he wanted to tell them. Any change to the plan represented a risk. The comfort she felt was interesting, because in the period of about a day she'd begun to depend on him and trust him to keep her safe. It made her a little mad at herself. She was usually so independent and didn't like relying on someone as she did with Vince right now. It made her understand the trust others placed in him a little better. In a moment of introspection, she contemplated what an odd mixture of feelings he inspired. Her mind was spinning on topics she couldn't solve. She shook her head and focused on the present and chalked it up to the situation and something she could ponder another time. Any deviation from the plan caused anxiety, but something about Vince made people feel safe. Well, as safe as possible with all that was going on.

Vince stepped into the middle of the group, and everyone focused on him and stopped talking among themselves. "Junior and Malcolm, you can come in close enough to hear, but I need you to keep your backs to me and eyes facing out please," he said. "Safety first. The same for you and the road, Dwight, if you don't mind."

Dwight gave a firm nod. "Roger that."

"There is nothing to worry about, so let's dispel that right away. The good news is that I ran into a community of solid people defending their homes and fields. Finding good people banding together is very good for us and the country."

"So why did we stop?" Liz asked. Vince understood Liz better by now and realized she wasn't challenging his decisions as some might assume; she was extremely inquisitive.

"Those people asked that we not travel through their community. They don't know us and are very wary of strangers."

"Couldn't we pay them, Vince?" Desperation tinged Liz's words.

"I considered it. I was in the midst of working that out when I realized they were only scared and wanted to be safe. To be honest, when I saw that, my heart wasn't in it."

"So where does that leave us?" Liz asked. "Won't we be less safe while we're respecting their community and safety?"

"Not at all. One of the men showed me a way around the community on the map. It may add a little to our time getting to French Lick. However, I think it's fine because of the added safety factor."

"What's the added safety factor?"

"I'll know the roads to our right are clear and protected by that farming community. We can move faster with not needing to check a bunch of those side roads," Vince said, trying to inspire confidence in them. "I wanted you all to stop so I could talk to you in person about my reason for this bypass route I want the drivers to take. Besides, I knew people must need a pee break and a chance to get a bite to eat. I know I did," he said with a smile meant to relax them.

DAVE

Dave walked back into the cabin from a short hiking trip in the mountains ringing the South Park Valley.

He hadn't realized how much he had grown used to having the hulking shadow of Levi with him until he hiked alone. He'd hiked alone for so much of his life he didn't expect to notice the absence as much as he did. In any event, he needed the exercise and the mind clearing that hiking gave him.

When he was back at the cabin and ready to work with Louis on some details of the company, he received a call from Vince. As unreliable as the phones were lately, it was better than the alternative.

Dave was relieved to hear that all were safe and headed to French Lick. Vince kept the call brief, not wanting to give away too much information. While perhaps they were being overly cautious, the agreement was to communicate infrequently and keep OPSEC during the calls so nothing would be given away that could allow anyone to use it to hurt them.

After Vince gave his briefing, Dave began explaining the good news about getting Levi into Kentucky as back up. However, the call was lost before he could get that far. He tried dialing back several times but couldn't get through.

LEVI

At about the same time, Levi was trying to call Dave with no success. He, Greg, Cami, and her little dog made the ride from Springfield toward Shelbyville, Kentucky, with no problems and were able to enjoy the trip.

As planned, they bypassed Shelbyville and went through Simpsonville, stopping at Greg's farm to spend the night.

"No use trying to drive there in the dark and getting someone hurt," Greg said.

Levi wanted to protest. He was eager to get to Carrollton yet he understood the wisdom in what Greg said, so he reluctantly agreed.

"Besides, Vince won't be traveling in the dark with those girls," Greg said when he saw the conflict in Levi's face. "If he's already made it to Carrollton, they're safe and you're not needed. If they haven't, they'll soon hunker down as well. We couldn't get to Carrollton before late in the night under these conditions anyway."

Levi nodded. "You're right."

"Now let's get some food in you." Greg was once again affable and playful.

"It's always about food with you," Cami chimed in.

When they got to Greg's place, it appeared to be nothing more than a gravel path leading into a pasture. After crossing a cattle guard, Levi saw several barns and some cattle. A couple of Greg's friends were living in an RV horse trailer combo beside the barn and guarding the cattle. The RV had a generator that they ran occasionally for power.

After turning right at the barn, they went downhill to a large country home with a pond behind it. There were a few cars parked there as well.

"I have a few family and friends staying with me, both for their safety and to help me guard the herd," Greg told Levi. "It's what you might call a win-win."

"Makes sense to me."

"One of the men is the Shelby County policeman I told you about. He doesn't stay here much. His in-laws have a similar farm a few miles away. He's making rounds between these farms and the city, trying to keep order where he can."

"We all worry about him a lot. We still have our church meetings," Cami said, "and we do a special prayer vigil for Jim and some others that we are worried about."

ELLIE

Ellie was concerned with how Kate and Malcolm were dealing with everything.

She supposed that level of worry was an improvement. Before now, she had been more concerned about surviving to the next day than being concerned about anyone's feelings. Now that she was more optimistic about basic survival, she had the luxury to worry about how Kate was feeling and how Malcolm was dealing with being outside his element and with her ex-husband being in charge.

Kate was a survivor. As much as she was missing Chicago and thought her world was crumbling around her, she would heal and move on eventually. Until then, Kate was too good at hiding her inner feelings. Ellie worried that wasn't good and they could come out later. It was a delicate process getting Kate to share her feelings.

Ellie moved to the back seat and got some alone time with Kate during the drive. Kate was more willing to open up and talked in the back of the mini-van.

"I miss normal things," Kate said. "You know I planned on being a lawyer. I wanted to work and earn the finer things in life and to travel the world. I wanted a nice home, a car, and shopping trips. I wanted a condo in Florida, or even some-place like Saint Martin, and ski trips in Colorado. I like my pedicures and social media and cable TV and smartphones. Mom, if this situation drags on for a long time or changes our lives for good, those things will never come back."

"I'm so sorry, honey. I never thought of it from your perspective."

"I want to experience the life you and Dad and Grandma and Grandpa did,"

Kate said. "I want to go to movies and dances. I want to be able to call a doctor when I don't feel well. I know I'm being whiny, but I feel so cheated."

It was hard for Ellie not to cry for her. Hearing Kate bare her soul made her heart hurt in the way only a mother could understand. Ellie was so angry at her generation for squandering the trust of the country and way of life for their children and grandchildren. This wasn't the time to tell Kate that life wasn't always easy or fair. She was right: the previous generation had ruined the sacred trust they should have held for the next. That trust was simply to keep the country's safety, wealth, and knowledge intact for the future. Any words of wisdom Ellie might have would be lost on Kate. She didn't need to hear it right now. They just hugged.

Life could sometimes be mean and had a way of teaching you hard lessons all on its own without pushing it on her right now. Ellie realized that for Kate and those a few years younger than her, this could be the hardest generation on children in a century or more. The worst part of it was that it could have been avoided. Ellie wanted to cry for the things Kate would miss. She thought about the friends Kate lost touch with and didn't know if they were okay or not. They talked about the uncertainty of whether life would get back to a semblance of what it was before.

As they were sharing these thoughts, Kate blurted out that there was a boy she was talking to in Chicago. Now she would never know how much he liked her or wanted to date her. Would she ever find a boy to date? Or would she have to be constrained to date the odd boy on the next farm over that was the only boy in her age range? Would it now be like some old fashioned arranged marriage?

All Ellie could do was hug and hold her tight. Her heart ached for her daughter.

Part Twenty-Four

NEW FRIENDS

"Sometimes good things fall apart so better things can fall together."

- Marilyn Monroe

LIZ

Vince took a moment to sit in the shade and have a bite to eat before getting back on the road.

Seeing him relaxing calmed the others a bit. They gathered around to eat as well. He sat in a position where he could observe the road through the trees.

Liz watched him eat and make small talk. Andy, Dwight, Malcolm, and Junior kept wandering in on short rotations to have a bite to eat, catch up on the conversation, and then drift back to the road or their assigned sector to watch for threats. She didn't want to intrude on his personal time with his men and family. When it was clear he was done and giving instruction to the men about the new route, she approached him and asked for a few moments of his time.

While the men were getting the vehicles loaded, she asked Vince, "May I ride with you?" She didn't use her flirting voice, although she did speak as sweetly as possible. "If it's as safe as you said, I should be fine riding ahead with you."

Liz was used to getting what she wanted. She felt cooped up and claustrophobic with the others. Vince was a man who was self-assured and in charge. She wondered why things hadn't worked out between him and Ellie. She wanted to could find a smooth way to work the conversation around to that.

"You're not trained in how to handle yourself in this circumstance," Vince tried to argue when Liz asked if she could ride with him. "I would spend more time trying to take care of you than doing my job."

"You don't have to worry about me," Liz countered. "Besides, you said this was a fairly safe stretch, didn't you?"

"You're a famous movie star. People would kill me if I let you get hurt. You have a guard whose job it is to protect you. I definitely don't need both of you riding up here on point."

"I'm not much safer back there with the group," Liz argued. "It's true that there are more guns back there, but there are more people to protect too. Furthermore, we're a more noticeable target with three vehicles that are so obviously well-guarded back there."

Vince prided himself on being a man of details and focus and always kept in mind General Colin Powell's words: *"Never neglect details. When everyone's mind is dulled or distracted the leader must be doubly vigilant."* Also, he still couldn't shake the feeling they were being watched. He had learned during his time in Iraq and Afghanistan not to ignore those feelings.

Vince didn't want the distraction, and although Liz was definitely a distraction, he was forced to admit she made a good argument. He wanted to get on the road, and she was persistent. Part of him enjoyed the thought of a lady who was so beautiful and sought after riding in his shotgun seat.

"Okay," he relented. "But you have to follow my directions."

"Yes!" Liz flashed her smile that melted the resolve of men around the world.

"I mean it," Vince said. "Once you get in that truck, if I say something or give an instruction, there can be no argument. You can't even hesitate. If you do, you endanger me and this mission and that means my family. I won't risk them. You'll go back to the other truck, even if I have to make you walk."

Liz's countenance changed and immediately became more serious. "I promise. I won't be any trouble, and I'll do whatever you say."

Had Vince not turned away for a moment, he would have seen a mischievous smile sneak across her face. This would be fun, despite all the death and chaos they'd been through.

As Liz reached for the door handle of the truck, Vince asked, "Are you armed?"

"Yes." Liz showed him the revolver, still fully loaded since the raid on Ellie and Malcolm's home.

"This is not a joy ride," Vince said sternly. "You need to be armed and ready to use that. Only not in the truck and not until I tell you. It's possible a situation could seem like the time for a gun and not be, so don't do anything until I tell you. Shooting is always a last resort. It's an act you can't undo. If you choose poorly, it only makes things worse."

"I promise," Liz said somberly. She didn't want to shoot anyone. After Chicago, she wasn't sure she could. While she had a burning desire to not be a victim like Jennifer had been on the trek through Chicago, neither did she want to be the cause of that happening to anyone else through her inaction. She was happy Vince was in charge and she wouldn't have to make those decisions on her own.

Vince was pleased that she was taking it with the seriousness it deserved. She didn't have the giggling attitude, silliness, or condescending attitude he might have expected from another of the Hollywood in crowd.

They drove off down the road. The group behind them would wait ten to fifteen minutes to leave so as to provide the gap Vince wanted.

ELLIE

When Ellie saw Liz get in the truck with Vince, she caught her breath for a moment.

Aside from some long looks or flirtatious women while they were married, Ellie never had to see another woman take notice of Vince. She surprised herself when she realized she was experiencing a small pang of jealousy about her ex-husband. It was silly, really; she was the one who asked for the divorce. Besides, she was very happy with Malcolm. Vince deserved happiness too, even though it didn't make sense with someone like Liz Pendleton. She was younger and a movie star.

After a moment to reflect, Ellie smiled, glad the people around her couldn't read minds.

When she was younger, she wouldn't have had the self-awareness to analyze her feelings and why things bothered her. Liz was a beautiful woman. If truth be told, she was one of the most beautiful in Hollywood. She had the acting skills to match the old silver screen stars. Liz didn't seem affected by the Hollywood crowd and politics. She was a good person and possessed an array of personal attributes that complemented her acting skills and brought her roles to life.

Moreover, Ellie knew that Vince was a hard man to get to know. Recognizing that Liz was several years his junior, Ellie decided she was probably only searching for the excitement of riding up front, seeing the action and talking to the expedition leader. She couldn't possibly be interested in a grumpy old war horse like Vince.

The more that Ellie thought this through, the more she chuckled inwardly. If Liz did have a thought of a walk on the wild side with an old soldier, two or three hours in a truck with Vince would solve that. She was certain Vince would never fool around while on a mission. When he was bored or had too much time on his hands, well, that was different. On a mission, he could be short tempered and cantankerous. For sure his political views and values wouldn't mesh with those Hollywood people. Vince was an attractive man in his way, though not in the category that Liz was used to in Hollywood. The thought of those two with their diverse ages and world views trapped in a car together and the resulting bickering nearly made Ellie laugh out loud. She didn't think Liz and he could have anything in common. In another time and place and with another type of lady, Vince could and would pour on the charm to rival many Hollywood players. Just not here and now and with Liz Pendleton.

It was very attractive in its own primal way for a woman to have a man like Vince around. It was just damn hard to live with as a mate. At heart, Vince was a romantic and as tender hearted as anyone she'd known. However, getting him to share that side of himself and trust someone was not an easy task. Vince carried too much on his mind from the wars and was too much of an alpha male to be the type of husband a woman needed when there wasn't a war to fight.

There was a chasm of difference between how Vince felt love and what he thought of as hunting or sport. When Vince killed one buck or played one golf course well, that didn't mean he wouldn't want to try and take down a bigger buck or play a harder golf course. She finally grew tired of waiting for him to grow out of this need for conquest.

After the divorce and marrying Malcolm, Ellie was able to assess who Vince was more dispassionately from a distance. Something inside of a man like Vince craved the hunt and needed that validation. While she was sure he'd loved her then and still did today, she was also aware there were times in his life when he was driven by the need to hunt. The right words and charm were much like putting out food plots or scent trails to attract deer. For him, sex was like the moment when a well-placed shot brings down a ten-point buck. At that moment, he was alive and primal. Ellie had gotten over her judgment of who Vince was during their marriage, because she had moved on and was happy.

Despite knowing these things about Vince now in an intellectual way, that didn't mean Ellie could live with it daily. It took a toll on a woman to wonder each day where his mind was, if he was bored or wanted more or was unsettled. That restlessness was alien to her as a woman. She wondered for a moment whether she should warn Liz away from him, then with a wry smile decided not to. Not because she was jealous, but because it would be a very awkward conversation coming from an ex-wife. By expressing out loud or assuming that a young Hollywood beauty would have a romantic interest in an older man like Vince would make Ellie feel more embarrassed than Liz. Besides, Liz was a confident, self-assured adult. She could protect herself emotionally if she did decide to pursue him.

LEVI

Levi was usually one of the first up before the sun crept over the horizon. This morning he woke to a home that was already full of activity even though the sun wasn't fully up.

Cami smiled when he walked into the kitchen. "Would you like some coffee?"

Levi gratefully accepted and sipped the coffee. "Do you know where Greg is?"

"He wanted to feed the cattle and check on things before we get going. He didn't want to wake you. He'll feel better knowing everything is done before we go. You were so tired we wanted to let you rest. We know you city boys keep different hours than we do here."

"I should've gotten up earlier. I don't usually sleep this late," Levi said, feeling a bit embarrassed.

Cami was smiling with a cheerful energy for this early in the morning. "It's okay. We knew you came a long way and probably had jet lag. No telling how much you needed to do to get ready for the trip."

"Thanks," Levi responded, still not feeling better about it.

"Besides, when you live on a farm, these are normal hours. People are used to it."

Levi grimaced. He wanted to talk about the early hours of a Special Forces soldier, although he was fairly certain the point he might have made didn't sound as valid under the current circumstances. He got a quick breakfast from Cami, then went out to find Greg. A few of Greg's friends were outside working around the house; others were at the barn with the cattle or in the garden. A friend of Greg's directed Levi to a large red tractor. Greg was moving a round bale of hay to a field with the cattle. A couple of the men were carrying rifles. Others wore holstered handguns on their hips.

When Levi got close, Greg stopped the tractor and shut it off so they could speak.

"I hate to push you, Greg," Levi said, "but will we be leaving soon?"

"Heck yeah!" Greg said with that familiar smile he and Cami shared in common. "I wanted to feed my cattle, and you needed your rest. I'm about done here, so we can leave soon."

"Thanks. Is there anything I can do to help?"

"Nah, I don't want you to get hurt. Besides, we're pretty close to being done."

Levi grimaced again. This farming work could hurt a man's ego if you let it. Even though he was from New York City, he was still a trained Israeli Special Forces soldier and had no reason to be afraid of cattle and farm equipment. He turned to head back.

It was at that second, inches behind him, he heard the loudest, ghastly sound that could only be described as a huge, breathy anguished *ehhhhhh ahhhhhh* followed by several short *ahhh's*. To Levi, it sounded like a deathly animalistic screech that could have been heard for a mile. Hearing it from less than two feet away about made him dive for cover like a mortar round landing close to him. If his boots hadn't been laced tight, he might have jumped out of them.

During his talk with Greg, a cow must have slipped up close behind him. Levi decided to stick to combat and leave farming to the professionals. He stomped back to the house to pack for the trip, trying to ignore the poorly concealed laughter of the men around him.

When Greg got back to the house, Levi asked, "Why are all the men carrying guns? Have you had much trouble?"

"Nahh," Greg said. "It's only that it's better to be prepared just in case. Jim is over yonder talking to some of the other men from my church group. He knows of some people who've been broken into or killed. My farm is too remote to worry much."

"Makes sense."

"Jim is a detective from Shelbyville, and a couple of the others are former soldiers. They insist it would be a shame to let people think we were soft or easy targets in the unlikely event they do come this way."

"Are you worried about leaving your farm to take me to Carrollton?" Levi asked.

"Nope. These men are better fighters and shooters than me. We're all in a men's church group together. A few of them are living here with me till this all blows over. They'll keep it safe."

"What if it doesn't blow over?"

"Then I guess I have permanent roommates," Greg said with his trademark huge smile. "It always does blow over eventually though, doesn't it?"

"Until the day it doesn't," Levi said under his breath.

Greg didn't hear the last part. "Cami should have some snacks ready for us. Then we can get on the road."

Part Twenty-Five

APPROACHING SAFETY

"Betrayal is common for men with no conscience."

- Toba Beta

VINCE

Vince was on edge, partially because he felt responsible for Liz, though mostly because he preferred working alone.

She was beautiful, and he was a grizzled middle-aged veteran and divorcee. Being around her made him feel backwards and self-conscious.

To his surprise, the trip went without incident. They saw farmhouses that appeared occupied and people working the fields. A man on a bypass crossed their path going the opposite direction. They passed a few people walking who reminded Vince of the tired, dispirited people he'd seen in third world countries. It was disheartening to see it here in the heart of America.

What surprised Vince even more was the conversation. Liz had a way of asking innocuous questions that were easy for him to answer. She easily kept the conversation going, all while scanning for threats and taking her shotgun rider role seriously. He didn't feel peppered with questions, nor did he feel like she was rattling on about all manner of things that didn't have any relevance to their situation. The conversation was easy, fun, and germane. When he paused to think about it, Vince thought that in talking to her he probably revealed more about himself to her than he had to anyone in a long time. He hadn't meant to share that much and was surprised he didn't feel self-conscious about it either.

LIZ

Liz always thought that a huge factor in her success as an actress was her understanding of people at a very basic level. She loved people for all their qualities, flaws and all.

Liz loved the old fishermen on the dock in San Francisco. She loved the oil tycoon's wife and the immigrant who cleaned offices at night, not on a personal level but as real "people," who had a story and minute mannerisms that differentiated them from all others. She was a collector of stories, mannerisms, and a mimic of many of those personalities and traits. When she was in front of the camera, she drew on those people and collected back stories and behaviors to quilt together a performance that met the writer's expectation. Liz possessed a special skill to combine the words given to her by an author and the character she created from her collection into a believable and three-dimensional performance for the theatergoer.

She had always done this naturally. She didn't know how other actors did it. She didn't ask. It was a very private part of who she was. A few years back, she read a quote from Clint Eastwood that made her feel validated in the way she did this. *"You spend your life training to be an actor, observing people's characteristics so that you can design characters around what you've seen."*

Vince was different than most any other man she'd met. Each time she expected his story to go one way, his answer would surprise her. When she thought she had him pegged, something different would come out. She tried to shock him or get a rise out of him with a few statements, and his responses were not what she expected. The same held true for his mannerisms, which were one way when around his daughter, another around the men, and totally different when scanning for trouble. His whole persona could change at a moment's notice with no residual trace of who he had been a moment before.

Liz took note that those mannerisms were different when he was alone with her rather than when he was around the others. She was sure he didn't even notice he was acting differently. Vince might be a good poker player, but he had some very strong "tells" that Liz was quick to pick up on. Occasionally, he would even relax, as if he was about to flirt. Then at a moment's notice it was as if a shield came up and he would be all business.

Although she experienced way too much death and chaos on this trip, right now it was fun. As she leaned back in her seat and smiled, she saw him raise an eyebrow and glance at her quizzically.

ELLIE

As they got closer to French Lick, Malcolm said to Ellie, "We're going through gas faster than I planned. If I'm running low, the others must be as well."

"Are we going to run out?" Ellie asked, almost frantic. "Do we need to stop?"

"No," Malcolm said, sorry he brought it up. "We probably have enough. I'm going to shut off everything we don't need, though, and drive at a slow, steady pace to conserve fuel."

"Should we call Vince?" Ellie regretted saying it the moment the words left her mouth.

"No, we're okay for now. Vince wants only essential radio transmissions. If things get worse later, then I'll do something."

When Malcolm slowed, the other cars followed suit. It wasn't long before they came to the edge of the town of West Baden Springs. From a previous radio transmission, they were aware Vince was hiding in an alley and waiting for them to pass by going into town. He instructed them to bunch together, move faster, and have their guns ready when they went through congested areas.

In addition to being low on fuel, the van started running rough a few miles before reaching West Baden. Although Malcolm wasn't sure if it was the low fuel or some other mechanical problem, the end result was the same. When he accelerated a short way inside the city limits, the van sputtered and lost power. He scanned the area, searching for a good place to pull over. They were near a store whose sign advertised both fireworks and gun sales, of all things.

Vince had told him that if they had all been soldiers, they would have kept the convoy going and dealt with a stalled vehicle later. This was different. The van carried the very people and supplies they wanted to save.

Malcolm let the van coast to a stop in the store's parking lot while flashing his lights at the other cars. The other vehicles hastily pulled off in order to protect Malcolm's van and the people in it. While Malcolm was stressed about the vehicle giving out, he hooted at the irony of a store that sold both fireworks and guns. Perhaps it was stress catching up with him. He burst out laughing, and Ellie stared at him as if he'd lost his mind. He wasn't paying attention to Ellie but rather the silly sign and the store that had been looted and burned. *Guns and Fireworks!*

Vince circled back to the group. They hastily began moving the gear and supplies to the other vehicles so they could make it to Gus's place. While they were doing that, they began taking rifle fire from a distance. Vince was pretty sure it wasn't a heavy caliber round. He thought it might have been a .556 from an AR rifle. He was sure it wasn't the subsonic sound of a 9 MM, and it didn't have the deeper sound of a .308, 30-30 or .30-06. It didn't matter. If a round hit a person, the results were bad either way. The shots appeared to be coming from the parking lot of a visitor's center at the entrance to the West Baden Springs Hotel and Arboretum. Everyone was quick to get behind something solid. Andy and Dwight returned fire to make the shooter keep his head down. Vince couldn't tell if this was a serious threat they needed to fort up and go handle or if it was some local thug taking a few potshots. In the interest of speed, he decided to escape and evade this time. They needed to get to Gus's. It would be foolish to stop and engage the shooter. Right now, the shots were not accurate or well-aimed. That would change if they didn't get a move on soon.

Andy and Dwight fired a few more retaliatory shots back at the visitor's center to make the shooter duck and give him something to think about. They threw the last items in the truck and got moving fast. Vince led them through a zigzag course of the narrow streets of French Lick, the gunfire fading behind them.

The part of Vince that was a soldier and a dad wanted to go back and find the shooter. Something about that didn't feel random. Still, his first priority was the group. His personal agenda would need to wait.

MALIK

Malik pulled his knife out of his own gang member's body. He'd stabbed him below the rib on the back right side. Dark red blood poured from his kidney. Malik's other hand was on the hot barrel of the rifle to keep it pointed in a safe direction as the man died.

"Man, what'd you do that for?" one of the other men said. "They were broke down. We had 'em!"

"We didn't have 'em!" Malik shouted, spittle running from the corner of his mouth that had been so cool and calculating a moment earlier. "The most we coulda done is hurt some of 'em and take some of their stuff. That's not my plan! Besides..." He left a long pause, staring them down. "I didn't give the order, and I'm in charge here!" His voice became loud and shrill at the end.

———

Most of the remaining gang members snuck out in the night to head back to Chicago. Only Malik's trusted lieutenant remained with him. Tidwell Smith, whom everyone called Tid, was a small man with a potbelly, and sneaky. It was Tidwell that Malik was sticking up for those many years ago in juvie when he killed his first man. Malik preferred the story that he was a crazed killer instead of sticking up for a friend, and Tid played right along.

LEVI

Levi was once again riding shotgun in Greg's truck. Cami was in the back seat alone, having left her dog at home.

They eased up the gravel road and over the cattle crossing to Todd's Point Road outside of Simpsonville, Kentucky. To anyone observing, it was a pleasant country drive, nothing different from a month ago. Greg drove back roads and turned onto Highway 53 for a few miles, then onto Ballardsville Road. They drove the curvy, hilly country roads that were so common in the southeast. They passed old farms and miles of box wire fence topped with barbed wire.

Many of the farms and homes had the modern metal pole barns of various sizes that had been built by the thousands across the country because they were so economical. The soldier in Levi thought they would be great places to hide because there were so many of them that no one would know which one they were in. At the same time, he wouldn't want to have to defend one because they had few windows, and the thin metal walls offered no ballistic protection.

Soon they came to the small town of Eminence from the west. A police car and a few trucks were parked on the left side of the road at the old high school. There was a sawhorse in the road with a sign directing traffic to the parking lot with the police cruiser.

When Greg pulled into the school, Levi asked, "Do we have time for this? Are you sure it's safe?"

"We don't have time not to," Greg said soberly. "I need to know what's going on, and it wouldn't be neighborly not to stop. It would cause more suspicion and problems to try and pass without stopping."

Levi nodded, trusting Greg's judgment.

As Greg rolled up beside the police car, he lowered his window. "How y'all doing?" he said affably. "Sittin' out getting some rays?"

Before the policemen could reply, one of the civilians in a truck nearby said, "Greg Simpson, is that you?"

Greg shielded his eyes to better see who was speaking.

"It's Terry King," the man said. "I did some concrete work for you a few years back. Do you still have that farm over off of Todd's Point Road?"

"Yes, I do. Haven't seen you in a while, Terry. How have you been?"

"Fair to middlin'. Do you still rabbit hunt?"

"I do. I've got a couple of good dogs right now, but I'm always on the lookout for a new place to let 'em run."

"When this all blows over, I know a couple places we can try," Terry said.

"If it blows over," Greg said somberly.

"Heck yeah, it'll blow over," Terry said. "Criminals is lazy, and the government will send in the National Guard or something. They always do."

Greg noticed the policeman watching the conversation closely and could sense Levi was becoming tense about the delay. "So how are things here in Eminence?" he asked the policeman. "Any problems?"

"We have our share of riffraff. We mostly know who they are and where they live. The real problem we have is people we don't know coming through and causing problems," the policeman said with a glare. It was clear he was weary and wary. "We only have three policemen in the town, and we split it up into shifts. Some of the locals stay with us to add some firepower in case a carload of trouble-makers come through."

"Makes sense to me," Greg said cheerfully.

"So why are you out driving around in this mess?" the policeman asked suspiciously.

"I promised a buddy of mine I'd get this big galoot here," Greg indicated Levi, "up to a little village they built near Carrollton."

"I heard about that place. I may want to check it out sometime."

Levi leaned across Greg and said, "You'd be welcome any time. I know the owner, and he always likes good people to come around."

"I hear it's expensive if you want to live there."

"The details can always be worked out for the right people," Levi offered. "We do need to be moving on, though. Is the route open and safe?"

"My town should be okay." He once again sounded officious. "Still, be careful.

You might get a potshot, or if you stop, someone might try something. So move on through as fast as you can without speeding. If we hear shots, we'll come running."

"Thank you," Greg said.

"If you're going through New Castle, though, it's closed. I wouldn't advise going around it, either."

"Why is it closed?" Greg said, sounding exasperated. "I'd rather not go around if I can help it. Those roads are twisty one-laners that would be easy to trap me on."

"I should have said it's mostly closed to through traffic and out of towners. I'll write you a note saying we know you and you're from Todd's Point. That might do the trick for you. You're right, though. I wouldn't advise going down some of those one-lane roads right now. It might be safe, but if it's not, you'd be all on your own. You'd be hard pressed to run, and you'd end up fighting at the place they chose."

"Sounds like you've seen some combat," Levi remarked.

"One tour in Iraq and another in Afghanistan. I never expected I'd be protecting convoys at home in Kentucky from ambushes like I was over there." The disgust was obvious on his face.

"Well, we need to get going," Greg said, trying to change the topic. "Do you have something to write on for that note?"

"I'll use the back of a citation from my pad so they know it's me. I suppose they could think I got shot and had my citation pad stolen, but I don't think most criminals think that far in advance."

After a few minutes, with note in hand, Greg eased up to the four-way stop in Eminence and turned left headed toward New Castle. As they passed some closed businesses on the left and a Dairy Queen on the right, they could see people watching them. It was clear some were getting hungry and desperation wasn't that far away. Greg and Levi both wondered what this town might be like in a few days or weeks if things didn't clear up.

Even though it wasn't a long drive to Carrollton, the trip was already taking longer than planned.

Part Twenty-Six

FORTRESS

"*Everyone has his superstitions. One of mine has always been when I started to go anywhere, or to do anything, never to turn back or stop until the thing intended was accomplished.*"

- Ulysses S. Grant

VINCE

Vince knew that their luck had been too good so far.

Something was bound to go wrong. In the grand scheme of things, having a mini-van break down wasn't a big deal. The exchange was made as fast as possible, and the van pushed into some brush at the back of the gun store's parking lot to be retrieved later if possible.

After evading the shooters, they made the run through West Baden Springs and then into French Lick at dusk with little interaction with any locals. When they got to the heart of French Lick, the people of the city were nowhere to be found. While the town may appear abandoned, many of them were likely hiding in their homes. From here, they only needed to cut over east on Highway 145 to Hunters Road. When they spotted the collision center on Hunters Road, Gus's wreckage yard was only a little further up the gravel, tree-lined road.

French Lick was a quaint area that had first seen growth back before the advent of electricity. The area boomed in the twenties when the railroad brought people from Chicago for the resort and the springs. Vince remembered coming here with Ellie during the good times of their marriage to see the arboretum and stay at the resort. He would play on the world class golf course while Ellie enjoyed the spa. Later they would enjoy a great dinner at the resort. Sometimes Vince would spend a few hours at the casino cards tables while Ellie played the slots before they would go up to their room.

Few people outside the area knew how beautiful it was. Vince worried it would be one more irreplaceable thing destroyed during the turmoil.

LIZ

Liz was gazing out her window, scanning the area Vince asked her to as they went through French Lick and headed east.

They passed an automotive repair business, then went up a tree-lined gravel road. Liz saw a huge pile of junked cars scattered haphazardly the height of a two-story building at the top of a rise. The piles of mashed cars even covered the gravel entrance to the junkyard. To Liz's eye, there was no way in to the junkyard and nothing worth going in for. It appeared to be nothing more than junk, junk, and more junk.

Vince stopped the truck and opened the door. "Please stay in the truck," he said to Liz, then got out and walked toward the pile with his hands in the air.

"Stay there," someone shouted down. "I'm coming out."

To Liz's surprise, three crushed cars stacked one on top of the other swung out to the left. The pile was actually an overlapping wall, like a concentric circle. Within that wall where the outer layer surpassed the inner, the three smashed cars were revealed to be strapped on a forklift that was protected behind the wall. The forklift was driven forward to swing out like a door. Once the wall of cars was moved far enough, it created an opening that couldn't be seen unless you knew where to look. A person would have had to walk right up to that section of the wall and then turn to their right to notice an access point.

Liz saw Vince and an older man speaking. They were smiling, and then the older man patted Vince on the shoulder and invited him to follow.

KATE

On seeing the fortress of junk, Kate went from confusion to awe upon seeing how it was constructed and the ingenuity involved.

The caravan followed the older man in a golf cart through the opening into a labyrinth of junked cars to a metal building near a brick ranch-style home in the center. The opening was another concentric circle of junk that pivoted out enough to let them go in before pivoting back with the use of a forklift and junked cars strapped together.

From inside the walls, Kate could see observation platforms high in the junk that couldn't be seen from the outside. She could now see that what appeared to be nothing more than mounds of junked vehicles from the outside were actually walls of junk protecting an inner sanctum. Kate was sure she had only seen a portion of the inside of the junk kingdom. There were many sections and areas all divided by a complex warren of scrap.

There were more strategically placed forklifts at various places along the path. Although she couldn't be sure, Kate assumed some of the walls of junk were just that, while others were strapped or bolted together so they could be moved like the outer door they just entered through a moment ago. She could only surmise that certain portions of the network of walls could be changed to open and close paths and confuse intruders.

Kate was sure she heard chickens clucking, along with cattle or goats lowing. It made sense that they could create pens for livestock. If they had those, then they must have sections for gardens as well in the maze of junk.

The entire thing reminded her of the corn mazes her dad used to take her to on Halloween when she was young. The complexity and size of this was so much larger than anything she could have imagined.

If it were not constructed of junk, people would have regarded it as an inspired work of architecture.

MALIK

Malik couldn't go any further. He and Tid holed up in an empty hotel more than a mile away. It sat beside a creek well below where Gus's wreckage yard and business was located.

From studying the map, Malik saw the road dead ended, and there was no way out the way they went in. While he had no idea what they were doing up there, they had to come out eventually. If they didn't, he and Tid would go in.

"Those type people won't stay back there for too long," Malik said to Tid. "I ain't going in after 'em and getting us killed."

"We'll get 'em," Tid said, because he knew that was what Malik wanted to hear. He was scared of Malik. Even though they were best friends, Malik could lose his temper and kill anyone at any time. Except his brother Raheem, whom he had worshipped. That was why Tid knew Malik had to kill these people or die trying. Whatever slight hold on sanity Malik once had would fade away to nothing if he didn't. Then who knew what would happen? Whatever it was, Tid doubted he would survive it. He didn't think about that consciously in an intellectual way; it was more of an instinctive subconscious knowledge.

While they were waiting, Malik sent Tid out searching for food, women, or liquor. He wanted some time alone, and Tid was a resourceful man. He usually found something. Malik didn't worry about him coming back empty handed. Tid was sneaky and knew how to get things.

LEVI

Dave finally received a call on the SAT phone. He was overjoyed to learn that Vince, Liz, and the group made it safely to Gus's place in French Lick. The call was short and done in code-like double speak. They had no reason to believe they were being listened to. Yet why chance it?

Dave wanted to tell Vince that Levi was on his way to Kentucky, to be there to help if possible. However, because he hadn't heard from Levi in two days and didn't know for certain he had made it safely to Carrollton, Dave elected not to mention it. Vince had enough to worry about without wondering if his best friend was out there somewhere hurt and needing his help.

Greg eased the red Ford truck to a stop in front of a blockade at the city limits of New Castle, Kentucky. New Castle was a quaint country town that resembled a thousand other small towns across America. It would have looked natural in a Norman Rockwell painting. It was built on high land with a commanding view of the surrounding area from the courthouse or another tall building like the Christian church along Main Street.

Although Greg never let anything bother him, Levi was concerned about the roadblock. Greg lowered the window and opened the door to get out of the truck. One of the men on the blockade held up his hand in a gesture to stay put. Another man who was armed and wearing a bulletproof vest and military load-bearing gear moved to a position to cover the first man who cautiously approached Greg's window.

"The town's closed to through traffic and anyone who doesn't live here. You'll need to turn around," the man said. He wasn't rude about it but wasn't leaving the door open for questions or argument either. As he began backing away, Greg reach into his pocket for the note from the policeman in Eminence. Suddenly the man in the bulletproof vest moved to a few feet from the vehicle and brought his rifle from low ready to his shoulder, aimed directly at Greg's head.

Everyone froze for a few seconds. A couple more men raced from the blockade, yelling commands, and pulled Greg from the truck, put him face down on the ground with a knee in his back, while keeping guns trained on Levi and Cami. There was a moment when everyone stopped yelling. An older man sauntered out from blockade and announced it was his shift to be in charge.

He knelt next to Greg. "Greg, what in tarnation are you up to? You're too old to be wrestling with these young bucks. The way things are these days, you're lucky they didn't shoot first and ask questions later."

"Bill McMaster? Is that you? It's hard to see anything while I'm lying on my chest with my hands cuffed behind me. That young feller's kind of strong," Greg said, once again smiling. "You think he might undo me?"

Bill motioned for them to uncuff Greg, and they walked a few feet away from the others to speak.

"Bill, we haven't seen you at the church men's group in over a year," Greg said straightaway.

"I don't have much of an excuse. It's a bit of a drive over to Shelbyville, and I stay busy with these Rocky Mountain horses. I know I should get over there more often," Bill said sheepishly.

"Heck, Bill," Greg teased, "those horses ain't nothing more than big ole dogs. Those are about the friendliest horses the good Lord ever made. I know they're comfortable and will go anywhere. I just can't make myself ride 'em, though."

"Well, why not?" Bill said, sounding offended and already having forgotten they are at the blockade.

"'Cuz," Greg said with a gleam in his eye, "when they look at me with those big ole puppy dog eyes and lean their head on my shoulder to be petted, I feel like I'm climbing up on the back of an old Labrador retriever. That just don't seem right to me."

By this time, Bill knew Greg was teasing him. He shook his head and moved the topic back to the blockade. "So what are you doing out driving? You ought to be at home hunkered down and taking care of your cows."

"I would, and some of the other men from the church's men's group are staying with me for a while. But that big ol' boy in the passenger seat flew all the way here from Colorado. He needs to get to Carrollton. I said I'd take him, and here we are."

"Why do you have to take him?" Bill asked. "Why can't he take himself?"

"He's a good friend of Vince Cavanaugh. Vince's stepdaddy was my best friend, and Vince is now my buddy too. Besides, Cami wants to go see that town they're building on the hill near Carrollton. I promised I'd take her out to dinner there too."

"Well, the town is closed. You can't go this way, and the way around is dangerous."

"I was thinking about that while that big ol' boy was kneeling on my back." Greg eyed the man who pushed him on the ground a moment ago. "I have a note from a policeman in Eminence that the sheriff here needs to see, and this galoot here with me may have some news from outside the state that the sheriff needs to hear. So it's your duty to take us to the sheriff to be checked out. You can vouch for us being safe at least that far."

"It doesn't matter," Bill said. "He won't let you through. He's promised the citizens and blocked so many of their friends and others. He can't make an exception for you."

"I don't expect him to." Greg grinned. "He has to be a man of his word or people won't follow him. On the other hand, I do think he will want to read my note and hear what Levi there has to say." Bill started to speak, but Greg held up his hand. "When the sheriff hears us out, you and he can make a big 'to do' about kicking us out of town and how the sheriff won't change his rules for nobody."

"Okay," Bill said. "How does that help you all, though?"

"You need to make sure you're the one in charge of kicking us out is all. Then you do it on the other side of town."

Both men walked back to the blockade smiling.

"We need to escort these people to the sheriff," Bill said officiously to the men working the blockade. "I know he will kick them right out of town, but the driver has a message from Eminence for the sheriff, and the passenger has a message from out of state."

After some time in the courthouse and a very public display of being kicked out of town, they were once again headed north on Highway 55 headed toward Carrollton.

Part Twenty-Seven

SHOWER AND FOOD

"In prosperity our friends know us; in adversity we know our friends."

- John Churton Collins

VINCE

When they got to the center of the maze, Gus's home and office building came into view. Vince recognized the structures immediately. The surroundings were much different than the last time he was there. Last time, he'd been able to drive right up to the office. The construction of this labyrinth encircling the kingdom of junk in such a short amount of time was no small feat.

The tilled garden beside the house had been there before. The smell of pigs may have been there before as well; he couldn't be sure.

When they parked and exited the vehicles, Gus's wife Mary was on the front porch to greet them with an offer of a shower and a meal, neither of which could be more appreciated.

"I've only got two spare rooms in the house. You women can take those, though you might have to share a bed or use a cot because we're short on both. You men can bunk in the office building after dinner's over."

Dinner was simple and delicious. Mary made fried chicken and meatloaf, as well as green beans and mashed potatoes. She also made whole onions cooked in the stove the way Vince remembered Ellie loved, wrapped in tinfoil and baked until they were soft and eaten with a chunk of butter pushed into the middle. To the travelers, it was a feast. Gus was proud to admit that with the exception of the butter and meatloaf everything was raised inside what he called his fortress of junk. He even boasted that the meatloaf was ground deer meat mixed with regular hamburger to stretch the beef they had and make it taste more like ground beef.

The dinner conversation began with Vince's exclamation on all the change accomplished in only a few short days. Gus responded by proudly describing how he, his sons, and a few other family members had been working like an ant colony to construct their bug-in location.

"Vince, when you came through last time, it didn't seem like much yet because we'd mostly been working on the back forty. I knew things were getting worse in the country. If I was wrong, it might not have been good for business to cover the shop with my fortress of junk."

"It sounds like you've been planning this a long time."

"I guess. It's more like a silly dream. The grownup version of a fort building," Gus said modestly. "Many men look at the world and think 'what if...'"

"That's true."

"Well, in my case I'm not a woodsman who can hide in a cabin and feed my family with my skills at hunting and gathering. I'm not the soldier you are that can save and protect people with those skills and strategy."

"I didn't save them all," Vince said under his breath.

Gus kept talking, having not even heard Vince. "I'm not the visionary that your uncle is. He can build whole communities. I'm a simple man with my junk fortress in the country. I can make it not appear worth attacking for most of the crooks. For the few who do try me, I can make that attack so costly it's not worth it."

"I can see that," Andy gushed.

"Even more than that, I have gardens, crops, and livestock. If this goes on, over time I may invite a few trusted families here to help man the walls and tend the crops. I even have plans for a church and a school if we need them." Gus beamed with pride.

"You'd always be welcome at any of the charter towns. I know Uncle Dave would want me to try and convince you to come."

"I know, and I thank you and him both for the offer. You have to understand that in my eyes, this place is equally as grand and strong as what you all have down in Carrollton. And because I'm hiding behind junk, I'm less of a target than you. Even more important is that I'm at home. My home!"

"Well, I know you know this: you need to make sure you don't invite too many people or let yourself appear too comfortable. Then you might end up being a target for a bigger force than you're prepared for," Vince warned.

"I'll keep that in mind."

The dinner table got quiet, weighted by the heavy conversation. In an effort to lighten the mood, Liz jumped in. "How long have you been planning your fortress, Gus? It's fabulous."

"It's been on my mind for years," Gus said with pride.

"This has been mostly a fancy of mine until recently. All the prepping over the last few years gave me an excuse to do what I wanted to do anyway."

"I'm glad you finally admitted that, old man," Mary teased with mock severity.

Gus smiled, put his hand on top of hers on the table, and squeezed it. "When the prepping thing became more popular and the country got closer to some type of catastrophe, I got serious about creating my bug-in prep site here."

"Bug in?" Liz queried.

"That's when someone creates a defensible location at their own home with food and supplies for an extended period of time," Kate explained. "Most people live too close to population centers for that to be practical, so they bug *out* to a safer, less populated place."

"Why is it so important to get away from people?" Liz asked

"People are the most dangerous thing on this planet," Vince stated. "We create most all the heartache and pain in this world. All of our issues are self-imposed. The high population density areas are the worst."

"Why are the high-density areas the worst?"

"It's hard to put into words," Vince admitted. "People in the cities are like the cattle Gus has in pens out back. They've lost their ability to provide for themselves. They have very little knowledge of where things come from or how. They've lost their ethics and religion for the most part and have been taught to prey on each other."

"It can't be that bad," Liz said

"For those people, their food is trucked in loaded with chemicals. Their information is controlled by political parties and only a few news sources. The financial system they are a part of is a sham to keep them under control and just prosperous enough to not fight back for change," Vince explained, getting more passionate about the topic.

"People can't be that naïve."

"You're right, all the people all the time are not that naïve," Vince said. "It's the people who control the food, information, and finances that have been practicing the art of manipulation on a grand scale for centuries. They know the art of mass psychology on a scale that rivals most paranoid conspiracy theorists' thoughts. In this case, truth is stranger than fiction. They know that by belittling and encouraging the rejection of religion and ethics, the masses are more willing follow the program as long as they are given cell phones, cable TV, air conditioning, and other pleasures. When morality, ethics, and religion are strong, those things don't offer as much to people, and they are harder to control."

"Surely people know that's happening, if indeed it is," Liz said skeptically.

"Thousands know, maybe even millions. Those people move to the country or practice prepping or unfiltered religion. The rest are content to accept a way of life that makes them easier to manipulate."

"So are you saying all people in the cities are corrupt?"

"Not at all. I know a lot of great people who are very moral in the cities," Vince countered. "It's only that you have to be so much stronger ethically in the cities when you're surrounded by the propaganda daily like water torture. Mass psychosis is much easier to control and plan in the cities because people feed off of each other. Food and news that has been corrupted to serve their needs and not ours is easier when you send it to a single location like a cattle pen. That's why we gather cattle to feed them or give them medicine.

"When things get bad like now, and the food, fuel, and news stops flowing, those people will first scour the city and kill and ravage. You'll have a lot of hungry, unethical people ready to lie, cheat, and kill for a can of beans. That means it's not a safe place to bug in because the odds are so overwhelmingly stacked against you."

Liz wasn't convinced. "You make all cities sound like a Sodom and Gomorra hellhole."

"Well you just fought your way out of Chicago," Vince reminded her. "What do you think? I'm not saying it's all bad all the time, but under these circumstances, perhaps you're closer to the truth than you know."

Vince glanced over and saw Malcolm staring down at his plate. Many of Vince's points, although intended for Liz, hit home with Malcolm. "Malcolm down there at the end of the table is what's good about the big cities," Vince said.

Malcolm peered up at Vince questioningly.

"I am not backing away from what I just said. I still believe it to be true. However, keeping all that in mind, think about the inner strength of character and morality it takes to live your life and become the kind of man Malcolm is when surrounded by many who aren't. Malcolm and Raheem were raised in similar circumstances in the same neighborhood, and they turned out totally different."

"I did have my dad," Malcolm said. "And don't forget the other good people in the cities. Men like Mr. Goldberg who gave his life for us."

"You're right. Although you can't lose track of the fact that the people who control the news, food, and cities are masters of the tipping point thought process. For them, it's okay to have a few Malcolms and Mr. Goldbergs as long as they are kept well outnumbered." An awkward silence ensued, and Vince suspected he'd said too much.

Gus decided to change the subject and jovially filled the dead silence at the table. "For years I didn't share with hardly anyone, even my own family, my idea of a junk fortress. I figured they'd think I was nuts. This whole complex is like a maze now, and only a few of us know all the paths. To add to that, I've set it up so I can change the paths from time to time or block them if I choose. I even have some C4 under a few strategic spots to cause cave-ins that would take days to clear. In among those paths are the pens for hogs, goats, and several large fuel storage containers. I even have several of those huge shipping containers buried about the place with hidden living quarters, food, and ammo. We can ride out pretty much anything here. I have dozens of solar panels and some wind turbines atop certain junk piles recharging hundreds of recycled batteries. That's in addition to some large generators scavenged from a hospital and a computer company when they upgraded. I've collected junk anywhere I could find it through the years. I made a good living cleaning up lots of things. I have close to a hundred acres of junk here. I can make things and trade and hide and survive."

Kate smiled. "Wow, I'd love to see all that."

Gus smiled back. "I'd love to show you, young lady, but I suspect you need to get going in the morning. Keep in mind too, I don't show too many people, and almost no one sees it all. As long as everyone thinks I'm nothing more than a crazy old junkman, I should be good and my family safe and well fed."

"That's so cool." Kate beamed.

"You still do your other work too, don't you?" Vince asked.

"Yes, I fix up old cars. I have a side gig doing some up armor jobs on vehicles for certain clients. But like I said, if people think I'm a crazy old junkman who lives up in here with his guns, they'll leave me alone."

LIZ

Liz lingered in the shower longer than she needed.

It was a guilty pleasure she indulged in a few minutes longer than she needed even though she was aware that others wanted their turn and she didn't know how much hot water there was. It felt delightful to be human again with a clean shower and good food. Her trainer would sneer at the calories she'd eaten and question whether the food was organic. She didn't care right now.

Thinking of her trainer gave Liz a moment of pause. She didn't know what things were like in California, even if she was alive or not. Luxuriating in the warmth of a fresh shower and a full stomach gave Liz time to reflect. It was a wonder how time raced along in such a way that made recent events fade into memory so fast. In reality, it was barely a matter of weeks since things went to heck and she subsequently left the downtown Chicago penthouse. The old saying kept floating through her head, *"I'm exhausted from trying to be stronger than I feel."*

Because Liz had an eye for people and studied them, she noticed that when they were clean, fed, and safe, their whole demeanor changed. People spoke faster, smiled more, and exuded hope. She even heard laughter and a few jokes. It was strange to contemplate how rare and special laughter was. People needed laughter and joy so much more than they knew. It was definitely something that was taken for granted.

After dinner, they sat on the deck and listened to the sounds of the night. They talked, laughed, and joked. Liz found a comfortable spot on the step where she could lean her back against the post and gaze up at the sky, relax, and listen to the people around her. There was an easy camaraderie of shared experiences that reminded her of her grandmother's home in Kentucky. As the sky darkened and the conversation slowed, people yawned. It was clear the pace of the day was reverting to sunlight hours as it had been a century ago.

While some people wanted to stay up and talk, others made excuses to head to bed. Liz stayed to relish the feeling of being fed, clean, and safe. She chose to stay on the deck and enjoy a cool drink. She merely wanted to soak up the talk and friendship around her, sit and absorb it, and "be."

ELLIE

Ellie stretched languidly.

The bed felt great, and she would like to lie here all day. It was funny how much better a bed felt when she was tired or how much better food tasted when she was hungry. It was still dark outside and very early in the morning. She was filled with trepidation and wanted to bury her head in the pillow, enjoy the safety and comfort, and go back to sleep. She was scared about getting on the road again. When she got scared, it came out in anger or short-tempered responses to those around her. She didn't like doing it yet was helpless to stop herself sometimes.

Vince lived for this stuff. As much as he beat himself up over the losses and the imperfections on a mission, he was never truly alive with that pinpoint focus as when he was on a mission and living on the razor's edge. He was in his element whether he would admit it or not. She, on the other hand, worried and stressed. This was not the life for her. Ellie had no problem admitting that either to herself or others. She needed a sense of normalcy and safety for herself and her family.

Vince believed that humans were at their best when they struggled to survive, grow, and thrive. Other people had a lot of anxiety or stress over the struggle or conflict. They needed to be a part of something larger; they thrived on routine. Ellie was most happy being part of a team, a village, or community.

LEVI

Even Levi smiled when they were expelled from the town of New Castle on the north side, exactly where they wanted to be.

Greg's plan worked perfectly. His friend vouched for him, and with the note from the policeman in Eminence, the sheriff let down his guard and trusted them.

Sherriff Owens was gruff on the outside, yet Levi thought that was more from responsibility than his natural demeanor. He brought in food and spent a couple of hours grilling them about all they'd seen. At first, he focused exclusively on Greg, likely because Greg was a known and trusted commodity in the area and partially because Greg's information was more local and of immediate use. He wanted to know the road conditions, the responses of various small towns between Springfield and New Castle, and asked a lot of questions about his peers in other towns. When he found that Greg's friend and men's prayer group member was a detective in the Shelbyville police force, he asked about him too. Soon it was clear that although Greg saw a lot, he actually knew very little. That was true of most people not trained in observation. The government wasn't sharing much, and most news outlets were either uninformed or purposefully sharing stories so politically slanted that they had little informational value.

When Sherriff Owens got to Levi and learned his background, he became very interested. Levi briefly contemplated holding back. OPSEC was so well ingrained in him that he didn't like to share much. However, when he considered that he didn't know much that was classified secret information, he decided to be more open. The only portions he held back were things specific to the company, his mission, or where Dave got his information. Sherriff Owens was mostly interested from the perspective of trying to determine how long this crisis would last and if there actually was help on the horizon on a national level.

It soon became clear that there was nothing more to be added. Sheriff Owens couldn't suppress a smile when he instructed Bill McMaster, "Throw these people out of the city. Our closed city and the curfew law will not be circumvented just because someone has a friend in town."

"Yes sir!" Bill said, took them to the north end of town, and escorted them out.

Most of the rest of the drive was an uneventful trip through Kentucky farm country. The only moment of angst came when they traveled under Interstate 71. Overpasses and bridges created good ambush locations for attackers. Greg and Levi decided to hit it fast and keep their eyes peeled for trouble. In the end, nothing happened, and they were safely on their way and very close to the Carrollton charter town.

The Highway 55 route didn't take them directly through the actual town of Carrollton but bypassed it on the west side of the little Kentucky River, which was good because both Levi and Greg were concerned that with Carrollton's size and layout, it would be hard to police. They expected there would be a certain amount of chaos going on in Carrollton as in other cities of that size. Traveling up Highway 55 this close to their destination, they could occasionally see the Little Kentucky River to their right. "That's the river that joins with the mighty Ohio River that forms the northeastern border of the Carrollton charter town location," Greg explained. "Pretty soon, we'll see a low rise to the left and the Ohio River in front of us."

As they came around a bend in the road beside the river, Levi and Greg could see a new dock and a good deal of activity both in the road leading up to the town and in the smaller river. Levi spotted guards by the dock and at the bottom of the road from the town. Although they were trying to blend in and look innocuous, it was obvious what they were. On closer inspection, Levi recognized obscure guard platforms on the walls at the top of the hill as well.

Greg pulled the truck up next to one of the guards at the lower end of the road and said in a loud, affable voice, "Hi, we're not from around here. How y'all doing?"

"Hello?" The guard appeared a bit confused by Greg's loud and friendly demeanor.

"I'm Greg Simpson, and this here is my wife Cami. We're friends of Vince Cavanaugh's." Greg hooked a thumb to the passenger seat. "This big galoot next to me is Levi Goldman. He's a friend of Dave and Vince Cavanaugh both. We should be expected."

The first guard spoke into his walkie talkie, while the second kept his battle rifle casually pointed toward the truck but down in a low ready position. Soon the first guard turned back to Greg and said, "Follow me up the hill. I'll walk, so go slow. Welcome to Chartertown Carrollton."

Part Twenty-Eight

SO CLOSE

"Evil prevails when good men fail to act."

- Edmund Burke

VINCE

It was still dark as they prepared to leave Gus's.

They were back at full strength. The people and supplies were spread across four vehicles again. Gus generously offered them a repaired Nissan Pathfinder and said they could bring it back the next time they were up his way. He offered to retrieve the minivan and call it an even trade. Vince wasn't in a position to argue.

After they were loaded up and ready to roll, Vince announced to the group, "If we make good time and luck is with us, we'll make it home to Chartertown Carrollton tonight." As they pulled out of Gus's fortress, Vince looked back. It was still eerie seeing that pile of metal junk behind him move back into place. Even knowing what all was behind there, it was still hard to believe.

They made it through French Lick and then West Baden Springs with no incidents. From there, they headed east on Highway 150, which was known locally as part of Indiana's historic pathway. Vince reflected that if the situation was different, driving down a beautiful scenic highway with a gorgeous movie star beside him might have been a lifetime highlight. Under the current circumstances, it merely made him feel old and responsible. More like the designated driver at a bachelor party than the lucky guy who got a date with the head cheerleader.

They expected trouble at Paoli, Indiana. With no good way to go around, Vince decided to hit it hard and fast with each vehicle about twenty yards apart. With trained combat drivers, he might have chosen to bunch up the formation more. Vince wanted them to be close enough to offer fire support, however not so close that one big hit or wreck could pile them up. Paoli surprised them by being pretty calm. While there was some evidence of past violence, there were several people going about their business as they might have normally. It made Vince feel foolish to have run through their town like some convoy from Mad Max.

From there they kept heading east, this time on Highway 56. At Salem, Indiana, there was no good way to go around without losing a lot of time. On this occasion, Vince chose to go through first in a scout position. He saw some places where people were bartering like it was a flea market. A few people tried to wave him down. Vince wasn't sure why or what they thought he might have to trade. He made sure they could see he was armed and not stopping.

In her best Hollywood brat voice, Liz giggled and said, "We can't possibly stop. I don't see a Christian Louboutin booth. That's simply barbaric."

Surprising himself, Vince laughed with her. He radioed back to the other vehicles and told them to stay fairly close to each other this time and not race through town, although not to go slow enough to allow anyone to stop them, either. He broke his own radio protocol to say very clearly, "It's important that no matter what you see, do not stop for anything."

He previously warned them to be careful of the Walmart. It had clearly seen violence and looting, although now there were a lot of people camped out peacefully and trading. There was also a police presence in the massive parking lot. Even though that police presence and order could be a good thing, Vince didn't want their group getting caught up in it. Right now, crowds represented danger for them. A policeman might be corrupt or might detain them for a day to ask questions about where they'd been or what they'd seen.

Vince parked his vehicle at the intersection of Jim Day Road and Highway 56, making sure he was behind a large, abandoned tractor trailer and positioned a little past the Walmart where he could watch, and he waited. He wanted his group to make it past here fast and get through before people took much notice of them.

He hadn't realized he was holding his breath until his people passed. He pulled out behind them and let out a huge exhale of air from deep in his lungs. He glanced over to find Liz had been watching him intently the whole time.

Vince didn't want to test their luck a third time at Scottsburg, Indiana. The town was larger, and there was a perfect ambush site as they went under Interstate 65. He pulled ahead of the other vehicles and asked Liz to contact them on the walkie talkie to let them know he wanted them to prepare for a detour.

Vince wasn't sure why he didn't trust Scottsburg. Nevertheless, he had enough time in warzones to trust his instincts. If he was wrong, all it did was lengthen their drive some. If he was right and didn't follow his instincts, the results could be catastrophic. He was a strong believer in the ability of the mind to assimilate hundreds of tiny facts into a mental picture or instinct. Just because at a moment's notice you couldn't recall everything you had observed to create that instinct didn't mean it wasn't valid.

On the outskirts of Scottsburg, Vince turned right on Boatman Road and headed south. Liz passed on the commands for the detour change to the rest of the group in the cryptic language they were all using. Vince took note that she was getting good at it and her confidence was growing.

He was trying to find a road called Leota that would take them over Interstate 65 in a place that was very unlikely to be guarded. That route would then take them on to Highway 356. After pausing to go over the map, Vince decided they would stay on 356 all the way to where it, Highway 62, and their original route of Highway 56 came together. Highway 356 was a small country road that came with its own risk. It would be easy to blockade or set an ambush if someone wanted, even though unlikely on this route. Few people used this road, and because the route was not one that people would normally use, Vince didn't think it would be a likely choice for most bandits. They were far enough in the country that the people who lived there wouldn't allow thieves and bad people to set up shop in their area.

On Highway 56 a little ways past Thompson Road and before they got to the town of Hanover, Indiana, their luck ran out. There was a large crash scene involving semi-trucks that didn't appear to be totally accidental, effectively blocking the road. Some of the trucks were burned, and to Vince's trained eye, it was more likely a planned blockage than an accident. That thought was confirmed when he saw two men holding deer rifles standing right at the tree line near the vehicle impasse. They didn't try to hide and made no threatening move toward Vince. For a brief moment, he considered walking up to them for a parlay. When he thought about the risk to the people behind him and the woman in the truck with him, he decided against doing so. If this was a planned blockage, then they needed to get moving fast before someone could come out of the woods or up from behind and catch them in a crossfire.

Vince spotted a dirt path around the wreckage that, if he were pushing his luck, he might have driven through, but the risk was still too great. Vince turned around and asked Liz to signal the convoy to do the same, instructing them to head north toward Thompson Road. The whole scene was odd because the men at the blockade didn't act threatening.

When nothing bad happened, it made Vince consider that perhaps they weren't bad buys and were merely protecting their homes. It was frustrating because Vince knew they were getting so close to Carrollton, and they kept getting slowed down. *At least that's better than getting shot at,* Vince thought to himself.

They turned right from Thompson Road onto Highway 256 heading east to Madison, Indiana. The houses and business became more numerous. Vince was again riding point position a mile or so in advance when he heard a barrage of gunfire. There were multiple shooters by the dissimilar sounds of varied calibers of ammunition. He quickly instructed Liz to make a radio call for the rest to pull off and park at an old barn they'd passed a ways back. The barn was overgrown with bushes and trees and a great place for them to hide and take a break while Vince figured out what was going on and what to do about it.

Ahead of the main group, he pulled his truck behind a couple of cars and a tree on the north side of the road where he could get a view of the firefight. "Keep your gun ready and stay in the truck," he instructed Liz. "Slouch down so you can't be seen, but stay high enough that you have a clear field of vision. And don't forget to watch your six, behind, I mean. When the action is most engaging to the front is when the killers like to creep up from behind." He locked eyes with Liz. "Promise me you'll remember those things."

She nodded solemnly. Vince nodded back. He needed to get moving.

Of the two houses near where he hid the truck, one was obviously burned out and unoccupied. In the other home, Vince saw a young girl peek through the window before her mother pulled her back. The mom's face displayed a mixture of resignation and terror. Vince had seen that look in the war-torn nations more than he wanted. He never wanted to see it this close to home.

Vince put his finger to his lips in the universal sign asking them to be quiet. He didn't feel entirely safe with people at his back. However, he went with his instincts that they were not a threat. He needed to see what was going on with the gun battle at the intersection of Highway 256 and Highway 56, which was right where his group needed to go, and they were running out of detour options.

He worked his way around the base of a huge tree with a child's swing in it, and he finally spotted the firefight. It wasn't his fight, but they were in his way. Vince found a spot behind the tree and laid his .308 rifle with a scope over a limb holding the child's swing to see the action clearer. It went against the grain not to intervene. He didn't know who was in the right.

After some observation, he determined there was an older man with a teen boy on one side of the road behind a pickup truck with a flat tire. They were to Vince's right on the grass beside the highway. To his left and on the other side of the intersection were three men howling and shooting without even aiming and a younger girl with her hands tied in their truck. It was clear they had the older man and the boy pinned down and were in no hurry. The rear end of their truck was damaged. The bumper and rear quarter were pushed into a shredded tire.

When the girl screamed, "Papaaaaww!" long and loud and one of the men back-handed her across the face, Vince knew immediately what side he was on. He had to help. Vince didn't think of himself as a good man. Even so, he always believed that evil prevailed when good men failed to act. He could no more walk away from this than he could stop breathing.

He peered through the Nikon Monarch scope mounted atop his Winchester SX-AR .308 and sighted in on the ringleader. When the shot was clear, he took up the slack on the trigger. The rifle obeyed like an old dog; the bad guy didn't. At the last moment, he moved to avoid a shot from the old man, causing Vince's shot to hit him high in the thigh instead of center mass on the chest. The boom of the .308 and the blood spray from a gaping wound in their leader's thigh shocked his companions. When one of them stood up above his coverage to see who was flanking them, the old man shot him in the neck. The third man walked down the street toward Vince as if he was drunk or on drugs. He began firing two handguns like some drugged-out gangster gunslinger. Few of the rounds even came close to Vince, although he did hear two pings against a metal dumpster not too far away. He sighted in and fired center mass at the thug. The big .308 core-lokt round dropped him where he stood without even a flinch or moan.

For a moment, Vince was back in the war. Hearing a voice behind him jolted him back to the present, and he spun, bringing his gun up. "You did all you could. You tried not to kill them. I saw you shoot the first one in the leg and wait to shoot the second till he was almost on you."

"Aww hell, Liz. I thought I asked you to stay in the truck? You don't need to see this."

"Yeah, I startled you, though, the big bad warrior, didn't I?" she quipped.

Vince paused, drew in a breath for an angry retort, then sighed and laughed at himself. He must be getting old, letting a young girl slip up behind him while he was woolgathering. "Go back to the truck while I get these bodies out of sight so everyone else doesn't have to see them," Vince admonished. "Please."

"What about the one you shot in the leg? What will you do with him?"

"He's a goner too," Vince said. "I saw the spray of blood that indicated I hit an artery. If he isn't dead already, he will be by the time I get there. So much for trying not to kill them, huh?"

He preferred that she thought that he tried not to kill the first one. It was best that she not know the places his mind went and the fury that raged through him during a battle.

Liz locked eyes with him for a brief moment in a serious way. "You're doing good things for people. Keep your head in the game, cowboy."

She turned and walked away, leaving Vince to wonder if her hips always swayed that way or she was just teasing him.

LIZ

Liz was beginning to like Vince in much the same way a girl might like the friend of her older brother.

He had a tortured soul. She saw the same things he did during the firefight and knew he did right. She could tell that the killing and the need for it was piling up in his mind and eating away at him.

This was a side of a conservative red-blooded American man that her Hollywood crowd would scoff at and never understand. He did so much for others and focused so much of his energy keeping others safe that he deserved a smile and a little emotional pick me up occasionally. As most women do, Liz knew when she was being watched. She put a little extra ka-ching in her sway walking away from Vince to the truck. When she was sure she had his attention, she glanced back and winked. Just enough to let him know it wasn't sexual, only fun, she giggled to herself as she moved the last few steps to the truck and got in.

MALIK

Malik and Tid stopped at the top of a hill to observe the shots they heard.

They worried earlier that they'd lost track of the convoy. The shooting helped them zero back in on their lost quarry.

They were too far away. The group was armed well and on alert now. They would have to bide their time for the right opportunity or find reinforcements.

Part Twenty-Nine

TRUST

"*Courage is a perfect sensibility of the measure of danger, and a mental willingness to endure it.*"

- William Sherman

LEVI

Levi was impressed.

He studied the walled compound on the top of the hill ahead of him and to his left, as well as the activity around the boat dock to his right. The dock was obviously new and was built so it could float up and down on the metal poles as the river level changed. He observed with anticipation the restaurant at the base of the hill that Greg mentioned earlier and Vince told him about. Although he should keep kosher, sometimes he cheated. If things stayed as bad as Dave warned, following his religious dietary dictates was going to become a lot more difficult.

As he entered the city, what Levi noticed most was the activity and attitude. Most places and people were hunkering down during this period of national unrest. Many people across the country were afraid and in hiding or protection mode. Only the outlaws were out enjoying the breakdown in law and order. Here people were industrious, working hard and smiling, the security people well-armed but not in uniform. While the soldier in Levi wanted them in uniform, the practical side understood the value in having them blend in. A well-armed and uniformed security team indicated something of value worth securing. The Carrollton site had the vibe of normal people protecting their homes.

The wall around the compound was perhaps fifteen feet in height, the gate decorative and made to resemble a subdivision entrance more than a security hard point. Levi knew there was reinforced steel underneath the decorative veneer. Inside the wall were guard observation platforms spaced at regular intervals. They were low enough behind the wall to not present much of the guards above the wall.

Additionally, Vince and Jeff had adorned each wall post with decorative planters that gave the wall a less severe appearance yet still allowed the guards something to stand behind and blend into.

Inside the facility were streets and homes, like hundreds of planned neighborhoods across the county. There were sections with different style townhomes, brownstones, and even traditional southern homes with lawns. There were city buildings and a main street with businesses and apartments. It truly was "Mayberry" behind the walls, if you added in a very diverse architecture of homes within the town grid.

Greg parked the truck on the main street. "Levi, do you need me? Cami wants to go to some of the stores and see what's open and what they have in stock."

"I'm okay for now, thanks," Levi responded.

"Well, we're off on a shopping trip then!" Greg waved and followed Cami to the main street.

A man who appeared to be in charge came out of the government building and spoke to the guard that led Levi and Greg into the city, then turned to Levi and stuck out his hand. "Hi, I'm Don Allen. It's a pleasure to meet you. The men from the gate told me who you are. I guess I'm in charge around here while Vince is gone. As soon as he returns, I'll be glad to give it back to him."

Don was a broad-shouldered, blond-haired, blue-eyed man. He was a bit past middle age, his shoulders were wide, and his belt was probably a few notches wider than he would have preferred. Still, he had a strong presence, and people naturally deferred to him.

Levi shook his hand. "I'm Levi Goldman. I work for Mr. Cavanaugh. I'm also a friend of Vince's. I didn't know he agreed to take on the leadership role here."

Don's face was stern until he smiled, then it changed dramatically. "Vince hasn't exactly agreed to be in charge, although everyone naturally looks to him."

"That's probably just because he's a Cavanaugh," Levi said, mostly to gauge Don's reaction.

"I suppose that could have something to do with it," Don said, unconcerned with being politically correct. "People would follow him in any event, though. I was an Army Cav scout, and I've been in big corporations. Some men just inspire others to follow."

Levi felt the same way about Vince and was glad to hear Don say it. It made him warm up to him. In a friendlier tone, Levi said, "No one can draft Vince into a leadership role if he doesn't want to be there. Maybe you should think about doing the job long term."

"I don't want it," Don said vehemently. "I like living here, and I'll work my butt off for my neighbors. However, I like them too well to lead them. Leadership is lonely. I don't want half of them hating me. If I lead well, half will hate me. If I lead poorly and they all like me, some will get killed if conditions don't improve. I don't want that on my shoulders either."

"Sounds like you understand leadership very well," Levi said. "Mr. Cavanaugh would like you."

"I take that as a huge complement, Mr. Goldman, thank you. I guess you can say I've been around and seen and done a few things. Mr. Cavanaugh reminds me of an uncle I have that I think highly of. I hope to meet him sometime."

"Hopefully you will," Levi responded and then asked, "So, what's the plan for leadership here?"

"The plan was to get this place finished, hold some elections, and do some hiring for critical positions. Most of the hiring has been done. We still have some work to complete on the town. Elections weren't scheduled for a few months, when more of the residents were here. In the meantime, everyone was happy with Vince. Since he had to run up north, a lot of people seemed a little lost, so I stepped in. They could have told me to shut up and probably should have. I think people appreciate having someone take point. That's what a Scout does, so here I am."

"That's what I wanted to talk to you about," Levi said. "Is there somewhere we can talk in private?"

"Sure!" Don said, happy to have someone else to absorb some the weight of the choices he was making. "Come on in the town hall."

ELLIE

The shooting was over.

The convoy came forward as Liz instructed, and Vince asked Andy and Junior to take perimeter positions well away from the group to watch for more trouble. Vince called Dwight to him; he valued his judgment and skills. He was a lot deadlier than people knew, and Vince wanted him close to both his family and Liz. Just in case.

As the group gathered around the damaged truck, Vince was already speaking to the older man, who was hugging the young girl. With him was a teenaged boy who could have either been his son or grandson. The boy was already working to change a tire on their truck. The older man alternated between giving the boy instruction and talking to Vince. "My name is Bert Hayden, and I live not far away from here."

Vince shook his hand. "I hope you're okay. I don't mean to rush you, but those shots will draw people."

"It will only take a moment to get the tire changed and the fender pried away from the tire enough to drive home. I don't know how I can thank you enough for saving my granddaughter."

"You're welcome. I couldn't have not helped. I'm sorry I have to leave so fast. I'm trying to get across the river before it gets dark. I know the route, and it's not far. I'm concerned about Madison, though. Anything you can tell us about what's going on between here and there would be helpful."

"You're right to be concerned. The road over the dam and spillway up near

Belterra Casino has been out for a few weeks, so you can't go that way. A barge from upriver ran out of control and took out a span of the road over the river."

"I heard about the spillway bridge damage," Vince said. "That's why I planned on crossing the river at Madison."

"I wouldn't if I were you," Bert said. "The new bridge in Madison is still in great shape, but the town isn't safe. I don't know where all they came from, but some lowlifes have been running amok in Madison. We've always had our normal criminals. On top of that, the meth problem and some of the crime related to that have been on a steady rise for several years. However, I don't think all the current criminals are local or related to that. I think they're imports from Louisville, Cincinnati, or Indianapolis. I guess it don't matter, but they're here."

"We might be able to shoot through at night," Vince suggested.

"I suppose that's possible." Bert nodded. "You and a couple of your men are pretty handy with those long guns. As good as you are, I wouldn't try it, though. Lower Madison down near the bridge is where the scumbags have concentrated their power. That bridge is a long stretch to run while you're being shot at. I'm not thinking you want to do that with the women."

"Well, I have to come up with something."

"They're not totally organized yet," Bert said after a moment of contemplation. "I think there are several different factions of crooks down there that are competing to one up each other in ambushing people, stealing, and raping. That could give you an edge. Y'all are well armed and might make it through. I'm betting you'll take losses, though. I still wouldn't try it if I were you."

Vince needed time to think and wanted to change the subject for a moment. "Is that how your granddaughter was captured?"

"Nah, it was stupidity on my part. We're from downriver a ways from Madison. A little town called Hanover, Indiana. It has a beautiful liberal arts college. You might not have heard of it unless you're a big fan of Woody Harrelson."

"I know of it," Vince said.

"Then you know where I'm talking about. After things went to hell, a lot of good people moved into the college campus. We set up some defenses and a farmer's market for barter. It's a good place to trade information and other things we need. Heck, we even have a guy catching information on the HAM as well as some on regular AM radio. You can't trust any of the news on the television any more, although that's been true for several years."

Vince nodded.

"The government is claiming they're going to get things back together soon. Hell, I'll believe that when I see it."

"You never know," Dwight said sarcastically.

"Anyway, those men you shot were trading at the farmers market earlier. We knew who they were and that they were drunk, but they weren't doing much harm, so we didn't think it was worth the hassle to run them off, especially if they wanted to fight about it. They moved over to talk to some young folks who were kicking hacky sacks and tossing Frisbees. I guess things like that are coming back in fashion without the internet and much electricity. So I went about my business and quit watching them that close. Then one of the boys rushes up to me yelling that they grabbed my granddaughter. I saw them tearing out of the parking lot in a truck, so my grandson and I jumped in my truck as fast as we could and followed. I was surprised that so many people just sat and watched it happen. Then again, this whole situation is still so unreal to most people. Folks have been trained to not get involved for decades now."

"And look where not getting involved got 'em," Dwight added. Vince glanced at Dwight, realizing this must really bother him. He rarely spoke this much.

"Anyway, I caught up to 'em and couldn't get them to stop. I knew it would be bad for her if they made it to Madison. So I pitted 'em like a Nascar driver. Then we commenced to shooting, and you came along. I can't tell you how much your help meant to me. I sincerely thank you. If there is ever anything I can do for you, please let me know."

"No thanks needed," Vince said. "We all have families. Thank you for being one of the good guys."

Bert nodded. "Well anyhoo, it's getting dark in a couple hours. You can't go through Madison for now. I want to feed you as my way of saying thanks, then you can plan your next move."

Vince thought about all that Bert said and decided to take him up on his offer. "Should we follow you back to the college?"

"Naw, there's another group of us homeowners that have a few homes on a bluff above the river not far from the college. There is only one good way in and out. We have that access road blockaded, so we're good."

"Sounds like a solid place."

"We'll feed you well." Bert grinned. "Because the grocery store is so far away, most of us already had full pantries and large gardens when things went a little crazy. When you add in some generators, solar power, and a little rationing and sharing, things haven't hit us too hard yet. Several of the men and a couple of ladies hunt too. We have a few veterans mixed in with the group so it hasn't changed our lifestyle as much yet as it has for others. It shouldn't be too big a deal for us if the government gets things righted soon."

MALIK

Malik watched from hiding as the convoy left the shot-up truck and three mostly dead outlaws behind.

When they were gone, he walked up, surveyed the scene, and focused on one of the men. Despite what Vince predicted, the man hadn't bled out and stopped breathing yet. He was trying in vain to keep pressure on the wound and stop his blood from pouring out of a hole in his thigh the size of a softball.

"Man, patch me up," he begged Malik. "My boys in Madison control all of the lower part of the city. If you get me to them, they'll fix me up. You can have whatever you want, women, drugs, food, whatever!"

"Man, I'm in a hurry," Malik drawled. "I don't want you getting blood in my car, and your truck's shot up."

"You need me, man," he barely whispered. "My cousin runs that crew."

"Okay, I'll do it," Malik said with an evil sneer. "Let's shake on it."

With that, Malik yanked the man's hand from his wound and held it until he bled out and expired. "What I don't need," he said under his breath, "is you telling one of your boys I left you here."

Malik took his bloodied hand and held it to the man's neck to check his pulse before wiping his hand on the man's clothes and casually walking back to his own car.

VINCE

Vince reflected that this tight-knit group of people near Hanover was how things were supposed to work. Although many people might have thought Vince was a cynic, that wasn't true. He believed most people were basically decent and wanted to work together for the common good.

That was what the charter town concept was all about.

That night after dinner, Vince was sitting in a lounge chair on Bert's deck. They were relaxing and sharing the luxury of a cold beer. He was watching the timeless tranquility of the river far below. Without taking his eyes off the river, Vince told Bert about the charter town concept.

"I heard about that. I was interested to learn more, although people said it was only for rich people."

Vince shook his head. "I assure you it's similar to what you have here. It has walls and a little more planning on how to make it sustainable for a long time is all. We want it to be economically viable for a whole community in good times and bad."

"Sounds great," Bert said. "I'd like to see it sometime when things get good again."

After some small talk, Vince and Bert settled into a companionable silence, watching the river flow by. It was too early in the year for bugs to be bad, and the sunset was a gorgeous mix of red and orange.

As he drained his beer, Bert said, "Highway 56 through Madison is totally blocked due to a huge pile up that hasn't been cleared. That's why I was chasing those scumbags who took my granddaughter around the long way up Highway 62. Most people from here wouldn't go to lower Madison the way they went."

"Well, I need to figure something out," Vince said. "It'll work out. The good Lord never promised things would always be easy."

"I've been doing some thinking on that. I've got an older 39-foot Sea Ray Express down there," he said, motioning to the river. "It runs well and should hold your entire group, if you don't mind leaving your trucks here till you can come back for them. If that place of yours is close to the river, I'll run you up to it on my boat. I won't go as far as Louisville downriver or Cincinnati upriver, but I'll run you a couple hours if that'll help. I'm sorry, but I can't leave my wife and grandkids for too long or take that big of risk in not coming back. They need me."

Vince didn't reply immediately. He desperately wanted to accept Bert's offer, even though he was aware of how big a risk the man was taking. "It would be a huge help," he said after a pause. "I'll take you up on it if you're sure it's okay. I know what a risk you're taking. I can't express how much we'd appreciate it. Although if you have any doubts at all about doing this, please don't hesitate to say so. I know we can find another way."

"No, it's fine, I've already thought about it. There'll be some risk going past Madison, but if we do it in the dark going slow, we should be fine."

Vince was warming to the idea. "In a fast boat, we could be there in a few hours. If we had to walk or take a route around Madison, going slow and loaded down with supplies, it'll take us days to get there. This group is drained physically and emotionally."

"It's settled then. I'll get you upriver in the cover of darkness," Bert said.

"We are going to a place a little bit before Carrollton on the river."

Bert held up a hand. "Oh, I've seen a mess of construction up on the hill from that spot, and I've seen the new docks down in the mouth of the river where the Little Kentucky opens up into the Ohio River."

"That's it," Vince said.

"You're right, that's a short trip unloaded. It will take us a fair amount longer loaded down. We'll have more people on the boat than it's supposed to carry. That means I can't run too fast."

"It's a risk we'll have to take," Vince said. "At least going slow will be quieter and leave less of a wake."

"Only thing is, we need to slip by Madison on the river when the thugs are asleep. Let's leave around three a.m. You all need a few hours' sleep tonight."

MALIK

Malik walked through the granite halls of the historic Lanier Mansion in the heart of lower Madison only fifty to a hundred yards from the bank of the Ohio River.

He and Tid passed guards at key locations like at a military camp, except the order stopped there. They saw a couple of drunken men peeing on the building and snickering with bottles of booze in hand.

A few yards further, both men exchanged a knowing glance when they heard the anguished screams of people being tortured, and the sound made Malik squirm. He had no qualms about torture and enjoyed handing it out. His wince was due to memories of his time in mental facilities and hearing sounds much like these as he curled in his cot waiting for morning. The difference was, in the facilities, the people were tortured from within; these were being beaten and tortured by their captors. Malik was able to make out the distinct sounds of the screams of women and girls enduring a different type of torture. The stink of fear mixed with alcohol, urine, and pot pervaded this place.

He met with the leader of the largest gang that controlled most of lower Madison, exaggerating about the jewels and other valuables being carried by Vince's group. He didn't need to exaggerate about the beauty of the women in Vince's group. He twisted an elaborate story of how the men from the convoy ambushed and killed three of the leader's men for no good reason. Malik embellished the tale of how large his group was and the value of cooperating with a large gang from Chicago.

Many of the people in this gang were related to each other in some way. They were mad as hornets to hear that outsiders killed some of their own men. Greed for the valuables and women also helped fuel their bloodlust.

Lew was a large man, and his lieutenant Javier was even bigger. More than anything they respected the fact that Malik didn't back down or have any fear of them. They chalked it up to him being part of a big gang and lots of experience. They didn't know of his mental instability and time spent in institutions.

"Your plan makes sense. I need to wipe out that place in Hanover anyways," Lew said. "They got a lot of stuff I want, and I don't need people thinking they can do their own thing without paying tribute to us."

"Yeah, but those hillbillies will run out of everything except for corn soon. That's why you need us in Chicago," Malik shot back, everything he said sounding like a sneer. "When the time comes for you to control a bigger area the size of half the state of Indiana, I'll send men by the dozens. Only thing you'll owe me is first trading rights in your territory at a good rate."

"Might work," Lew said. The plan sounded good. He didn't want to be taken in by a slick talker. Yet he couldn't find the flaw in the plan. "Let's focus on Hanover for now," he said to give himself time.

Lew and Javier wanted to launch a raid into Hanover right now. Malik understood revenge, but he was more of a planner in an animalistic way. He didn't care what they wanted; he needed their numbers. Malik only wanted to kill the men and take the women. He didn't much care about the rest. He finally agreed to split the women with the gang in Madison as long as he got first choice.

Tomorrow they would decide how to bust into Hanover and take it all over. Tonight, they would party.

LIZ

There was a chill on the river as they left Bert's place.

Liz was still longing for a few more hours of sleep. Recently she'd gotten even less sleep than she would have on her grandmother's farm. Still, she was as refreshed as she could be under the circumstances. After a night at Gus's and spending a day in Hanover at Bert's, she was feeling almost human again.

They worked their way down the steps built into the steep hillside to the docks far below. It was both strange and beautiful to see the mist hovering a foot or so above the water. Vince warned them all to be quiet because sound traveled so well on water. There was something about the early morning darkness and a mist-shrouded river that urged people to talk in whispers, whether Vince had said anything or not. The mist made Liz think of history and all the boats that traveled this river during the last two hundred years. It reminded her of camping trips to this same river a few miles down as a teen to make out with that boy she'd known in school... What was his name?

As they loaded into Bert's cabin cruiser, Vince instructed everyone to find a spot and try not move around much. He reminded them again how well sound traveled on water, especially at night.

"When it's safe to move around more and talk, I'll let you know. I can't stress to you how important it is for us to slip past the thugs in Madison. We can't risk being seen or heard. The boat is overloaded. Both the weight and trying to keep noise down will force us to go slow, although that has advantages too. If we went fast and hit a partially submerged log, that could get us caught. Anything over a few miles per hour will make more noise and leave a wake that would almost glow in the moonlight."

Vince spoke low and intensely, working hard to hide his agitation. He was worried it would get light soon. If the sun came up, the mist might burn off and they would lose their concealment. It was taking longer than he wanted to get everyone up and going and then down the hillside to the dock. After that, he had to get people into the right spots and life jackets on as many as possible.

While they left many of their supplies at Bert's place, they still carried weapons, ammo, and a few supplies. Most of the loading was left to Vince. Bert was using a fuel container on wheels to top off both fuel tanks. Although fuel was getting harder to come by, he said he had enough.

When Bert cranked over the twin engines, it sounded unusually loud, echoing across the river. Liz was convinced anyone within five miles could hear them. Soon the engines idled down to a low rumble and they were on their way, working slowly upriver against the current. Vince relaxed some. That didn't mean he still wasn't very tightly wound and on guard.

Soon they slipped by a marina a mile or so downriver from Madison. Then they saw a floating dock in front of the city. Bert kept the boat away from the Indiana side so they would be harder to spot. Still, he didn't want to get too close to the Kentucky side and be seen there or get tangled in debris.

They could hear music coming from the Indiana side of the river at this time of morning. It sounded like the party was still in full swing near the gardens of the historic Lanier Mansion. Occasionally they could hear screams that made Vince grind his teeth in anger. Liz thought that Vince was probably thinking about how close it had been that those screams could have belonged to Bert's granddaughter. If it could have been her, then it could have been Kate. That made Liz think it could have also been her, and a chill went down her spine. Vince looked over as she shivered, mistakenly thinking it was the night air.

It was when they went under the bridge at the east end of Madison that their luck turned sour. A drunk who was peeing off the bridge saw the boat. He was so far above the river that it was dumb luck that he saw them at all. If that wasn't bad enough, the man was able to see enough of the name on the transom to recognize the boat.

Both Vince and Bert could hear him screaming into a radio, "Lew! That old man Bert that shot your cousin, he's headed up river with a whole passel of people!"

It wasn't long before they saw a light go on at the floating dock in front of the city. Bert slowly turned his head to Vince, raised his shoulders, and nodded in the soft glow of light from the gauges and strips on the floor of the boat. Vince returned the nod, and Bert exhaled a deep breath he hadn't known he'd been holding in and pushed the throttles forward. The big twin engines roared. The front end rose and the rear end dug deeper into the water. Bert couldn't go much faster, with all the people and supplies loading his boat down. This would be a bad time to hit a log and tear out an outdrive. Even without hitting something, it would only take a little chop in the water to swamp an already overloaded boat. He couldn't risk it.

They could only hope that the men were too drunk or too slow to mount much of a pursuit before the group could get further upriver. They needed to put a lot of distance between them and the thugs in Madison.

Vince sent a couple of people below to stack some cushions and other supplies against the back and sides of the boat. It was probably a futile attempt to provide some level of ballistic protection, but it kept people busy and gave them hope. Besides, you never knew. If it stopped one bullet, then it was worth it.

Meanwhile, Vince made sure his SX-AR .308 was loaded and ready. He checked the spare mags to make sure they were topped off and found a good shooting position at the rear right-hand corner of the boat behind the transom.

Andy, Dwight, and Junior got their battle rifles ready, checking their spare magazines to be sure they topped off with ammo and easy to access. Each man made sure their firing locations were secure with an unobstructed line of sight that didn't come to close to their buddies.

There wasn't much else Vince could do. He could only try to make sure the other passengers were well protected below and behind cover.

Just as he began to feel optimistic that they might get away, the dawn finally broke. The inky blackness of night turned to a pasty whiteness of a mist-covered morning that was light enough now to see the activity behind them.

When Liz saw the grim visage on Vince's face, she could tell the hope of evasion was gone. His jaw was set into the mien of a warrior. They were in for a fight.

DAVE

The insistent ring of the cell phone in his pocket jolted Dave.

It had been so hard to get a call through, he'd forgotten it was there. Dave and Louis were going over some of the numbers from various projects in an effort to keep up with the numerous contractors at different locations without his full staff when the phone startled him.

The idea of paying them in commodities and supplies was a stroke of genius. There was also the task of procuring supplies wherever they could. In some cases, there were supplies available and no transportation. In others, it was the opposite.

Most of the people who would be coming to the South Park location were already here. The ones that weren't probably wouldn't make it. That wasn't true for the other locations. There were people showing up daily trying to trade jewelry, cash, and electronics for a spot in the towns. Although it was heartbreaking to turn people away, and especially families, Dave and the leaders in his communities knew that most of these latecomers were the ones who would have been mocking these communities a few months ago.

Louis stood to leave the room as Dave answered the phone. It was a frantic call from his grandniece Kate.

"Uncle Dave!"

"Calm down, honey, I'm here. Slow down and tell me what's going on."

"We're on the Ohio River, and they're following us and shooting, and I don't know what to do!"

"Sweetheart, stay calm. Is your dad with you?"

"Yes, but they're all shooting, and there are so many of them. Can't you help or send in some Special Forces or something?" Kate said, sounding desperate.

Dave could barely make out her words over the furious sounds of battle behind her. "Sweetheart, listen to me. Your dad *is* the Special Forces. He will get you home safely. He always does. I can't do as much right now as I could have a few months ago."

"No, Uncle Dave, there are too many men. No place we go is safe!"

It wasn't like Kate to whine. She was such a strong girl. It tore at Dave's heart to hear her this way.

"Really, sweetheart, trust your dad and do what he says, and for God's sakes, stay low and keep yourself safe, I've—"

Dave was about say, "I've got help coming," but the connection was lost before he could. He desperately tried to call the number back several times. It wasn't working. It could be hours or days before he got a call through again. He was frantic. He didn't know if Kate was shot and dropped the phone or this was due to the satellite problems they'd been experiencing for weeks.

Dave hung up and tried several times to contact Levi at the Carrollton location with no success. Aside from losing his wife, this was the most helpless feeling in his life. He calmed his breathing and tried Levi one more time. If he could get through, Levi would know they were coming in by river and how to go help.

As things stood, the last communication from Vince said they expected to be coming in by land, although they weren't sure when or the exact route he would take. He cocked his arm to smash the phone against the wall in frustration. He was rich; he could get more. Then he thought Kate might call back and set the phone down on his desk and stepped away.

Louis came back in the room, and Dave described what he just learned of the situation. Louis was worried, too. He had come to think of Dave's family as his own over the years. Louis suggested sending text messages both to Vince and Levi. "We may not know if it gets through, though. Many times, a text message can get through when a voice call can't."

Part Thirty

BATTLE

"Out of every one hundred men, ten shouldn't even be there, eighty are just targets, nine are the real fighters, and we are lucky to have them, for they make the battle. Ah, but the one, one is a warrior, and he will bring the others back."

- Heraclitus

ELLIE

Malcolm was up top with the men who were shooting. Not to take long shots with a rifle, but with a shotgun in case he needed to repel boarders. Because of his size and inexperience in this kind of fighting, he would only take up space down below.

He was muttering under his breath as he did sometimes when he was nervous. "What the hell did everyone think? That this was some pirate movie?!" Malcolm's running dialogue with himself would have been funny if anyone had time to notice.

Ellie was standing in the opening to the lower bunk area, feeling helpless. Bert was crouched low at the wheel of the boat. She could see the boats behind them. Two of the pursuing boats directed their fire at Bert's boat from afar while her people methodically returned fire. It was so surreal, like watching a movie.

The other boat had more men with combat rifles shooting. Bert's boat was obviously bigger, older, and slower. Ellie recognized that the men from her side could darn sure hit what they aimed at. In only a few minutes, she saw that the return fire from the good guys was hitting targets and doing damage. That fact alone was slowing the advance of the bad guys. That was no small feat in a moving boat shooting at moving targets that far away. They were keeping the other two boats at bay for the moment.

It was when Ellie saw another fast boat coming up in her periphery on the Indiana side of the river that her heart sank. In a moment of self-pity, she shed a tear that was a mixture of anger and frustration. They couldn't catch a break!

"Bert!" Vince yelled in Bert's ear. "Stay down and keep the boat moving! Keep her as close to the Kentucky side of the river as you safely can. Just not so close that we lose the ability to do some evasive zigzag maneuvers or hit something."

Bert gave him a thumbs up in reply, not even attempting to speak above the noise.

"If we can keep them at bay for twenty to thirty minutes, we're home free!" Vince shouted so the others could hear.

A couple of the other men dropped their eyes and glanced at him sideways like he was crazy.

At first it gave Ellie a sense of hope when she heard Vince say that, then she saw the expression on the faces of the men and knew Vince's words for the gallows humor they were. She didn't think they had three more minutes, much less thirty. She wanted to bury her head in her hands and cry.

When Malcolm glanced back at Ellie, she realized by his expression that he too thought they were out of time. And if by some chance they made it that far, their destination better have a whole passel of Marines to save them. Malcolm had seen too much of gangsters in his life and didn't think they would quit the chase just because Bert found a port. It didn't seem possible this would turn out okay.

Ellie smiled back at Malcolm, hoping to reassure him and give him confidence. Things always seemed to work out for Vince. He liked to claim it was his great planning, though she thought he was damn lucky a lot of time if the truth be told.

To make matters worse, they were now taking fire from all three boats chasing them, and Andy was hit. Even though it didn't appear fatal, it took Andy and one more rifle out of the fight for the moment. Vince took Andy's M4 and a couple spare magazines and handed them to Malcolm. He patted Malcolm on the back and gave him a thumbs up. "You'll do fine. Just point it downriver at those boats and pull the trigger slowly, one shot at a time." Malcom's body language suggested he wasn't as confident in his abilities.

There was a lull in the shooting. Some of the defenders on the Sea Ray were low on ammo. Vince sent his expended magazines down below for Kate to reload and pulled his handgun, a Springfield competition XDM .45 ACP.

As he was doing this, an open bow speed boat banged into the port side of Bert's 39-foot Sea Ray. Vince dropped the handgun. Rather than search for it, he grabbed the closest thing at hand, a boathook. He used the boathook to try and shove the other boat away. He swiped at the hands of the man who was grasping at the rail of Bert's boat and was shocked to see the scarred face of Malik reaching for him from the open-bowed ski boat. Malik was grappling with Vince from the other boat, leaving Vince no time to ponder how he would be down here on the Ohio River from Chicago.

He didn't have time to think back to all the incidents on the way from Chicago and wonder if Malik had been close. He and Malik fell into the open bow of the thug's ski boat in a life and death struggle. While they fought, the other man in the ski boat was tying a line from their boat to the Sea Ray. Neither boat could pull away since both boats were entangled in dock lines attached to the rails and entangled in the fenders. Both boats were slowing, and the men in the other boats were fixated on their struggle.

Vince and Malik were gouging and hitting, each trying to get to their knives.

Malcolm reacted promptly and stopped shooting downriver. He was trying to cut the boats apart. Somewhere in the shooting, Dwight had been injured as well. It took them only seconds to apply a battle dressing to the wound, and he got back in the fight. His shooting helped keep the other boats at bay to a certain degree. Although he wanted to help with the fight between Vince and Malik, Dwight was intent on making sure the others didn't think the Sea Ray undefended.

It was at that moment that Vince was able to pin Malik's knife hand while getting his own hand under Malik's chin. Vince was bending Malik's head backwards over the railing on the front right side of the open bow. Malik was still trying to get his knife hand free to stab Vince. Neither man was aware of anything going on around them. The rest of the world became a distant afterthought.

It happened so fast. Right as Vince was pushing his head back, Malik arched his back for the leverage that allowed him to free his knife hand. The maneuver worked. He raised the knife above Vince's exposed neck to plunge it in from behind. Ellie couldn't see much of the fight from her vantage, although she could see the knife raised high above Vince's exposed neck, and she screamed.

In that instant, the boats slammed together from the tension of the lines that bound them and the force of the current. For a brief moment, Vince saw the horror in Malik's eyes as the shadow of the heavy Sea Ray covered his face. An instant later, the heavy hull of the Sea Ray crushed his head between the larger cabin cruiser and the open-bowed ski boat.

Although he'd seen death in many forms, Vince was aghast at the sight of Malik's mangled head and the smear of blood on both boats as they swung apart. Malcolm yelled for him to jump. Vince grasped one of the dangling lines that Malcolm finally sawed through. He was dragged through the water as the ski boat fell away. There was a lull in the action as both sides stood shocked by what they just witnessed. It was a gruesome way to see someone die, even by people so accustomed to death.

Bile rose in Ellie's throat.

It wasn't so much the vision of what happened that elicited that reaction; it was the sound.

From the second step of the galley, her view was mostly obscured. She screamed in horror when she saw Malik's hand grasping the knife held over Vince's neck. At that moment, she was knocked off her feet when the boats crashed together. She heard a sound like a pumpkin exploding.

The other people on the boat let out a sound half between a gasp and a wail.

She saw the blood spray and Malik's hand go limp and knew what happened.

Later in her dreams she would wake to the sound of a large melon being dropped from a fifth-floor balcony onto pavement.

Ellie imagined she would hear those sounds in her dreams for years to come.

VINCE

Bert wasn't driving that fast.

Even so, he didn't dare take the time to stop for Vince to climb back aboard and make themselves easy prey for the other men still following. While the thugs were rocked back on their heels for the moment, they weren't giving up.

Hand over hand, Vince pulled himself up the dangling dock line until he could grasp a rail. He needed to be careful and not allow himself to dangle too far down the line toward the rear of the boat. He didn't want to survive the fight with Malik only to get his feet sucked into the propellers and mangled or cut off. His arms and body were as weak as a newborn calf after the struggle and then hanging onto the rope through the rush of water. He kept trying to swing his foot over the side of the boat and coming up short. Just as he decided he wouldn't make it and would have to hold on as long as possible and be dragged alongside the boat until they were in a safe place, a pair of strong hands grasped his arm and ankle and pulled him up into the boat. He turned his head away from the spray of river water for a breath of air and glanced up at the boat, only to see Malcolm with a huge grin on his face.

"Glad you made it back, my man. I wasn't so sure about you for a while there."

Vince sat for a moment, bent over and breathing in huge, deep lungsful of air, river water dripping from his face and clothes while he caught his breath and tried to slow his heart rate. "I wasn't so sure myself for a minute there. Thanks for the hand. I was worn out," Vince said between gasps, his head hanging down, for the moment focused on nothing more than the water dripping from him to the carpet of the boat. He didn't trust his emotions yet to face the group.

"Brother, we all need a hand sometimes. We've got to be there for each other. You've been there for us. Besides, isn't that what this whole community thing you all are building is all about?"

Vince didn't know why it should affect him so strongly. However, Malcolm's comments filled him with a fresh burst of energy and optimism. "You couldn't have said it any better. Thanks, man." He reached out to embrace Malcolm and pat him on the back.

———

Still wet and weary, Vince sat on the white vinyl boat seat trying to catch his breath. He was resting his forearms on his knees and hanging his head down, allowing the beads of water to drop on the boat carpeting. He turned his head slightly to the right, facing downriver. With the horrific death of Malik, there had been a temporary respite from the violence. The appalling way Malik died shocked them all.

Now, the pursuing boats were picking up speed and resuming the hunt. The group would soon be taking heavy fire again. Vince steeled himself for the oncoming fight. He wondered how much longer they could hold out. They were so close yet still so far from their destination.

He only needed another few seconds to catch his breath, then he planned to give 'em hell. He never believed he would win every fight. One day, the odds would be too overwhelming or a bullet would have his name on it. As a soldier, he had long ago come to terms with that. He only hoped that when he went to Hell, he would slide in on the blood of a lot of dead bad guys.

This was different and heartbreaking. In his worst nightmares, he couldn't contemplate the people he loved most would die or worse because he couldn't do enough to save them. He looked around. He could read the despair etched deep in their faces. They were injured, low on ammo, overwhelmed by men and firepower, and had just seen a gruesome death up close. At least the fighting would keep them from thinking about what might happen if they were captured. While the men had little worry of experiencing that, the women should pray that they never got the chance to learn.

Vince readied for the fight that was fast approaching from astern. Both he and Malcolm were worried about the thugs, the future, and keeping their family safe from two very different perspectives. Malcolm was a good man who lived his life honorably. Vince was a warrior. The difference between Vince and Malcolm was that this was Vince's kind of world. As good as men like Malcolm were, this was not a world for the good and honorable. This was a world for the mean and ruthless.

Vince was mean and ruthless.

At that moment, the beauty of what Uncle Dave was building finally crystalized in Vince's mind in a lightbulb moment. Decent, honorable men like Malcolm and ruthless, mean men like Vince needed to team together to shield people like Ellie, Kate, and Liz from the chaos and darkness sweeping the country. Calling these cities an Ark was a stroke of genius. They did need two of everything from auto mechanics, to doctors, to artists and poets. People like Uncle Dave could conceive the cities and fund them. People like Malcolm were the hardworking blue-collared backbone of these refuges. Vince knew that men like him would be the mean, ruthless bastards manning the walls and protecting it. Every time in history when a nation prospered, somewhere there was a story of a mean bastard on the wall willing to get rained on, maimed, or killed so people like Ellie, Kate, Liz, and Malcolm could go on living and building.

Vince knew he couldn't show worry and concern in his face and posture, because if he was worried, the rest of the group would as well. While he was trained to deliver and get things done under stress, most of these people were not. They needed to believe he had a plan and things would work out. His stress and worry was his burden alone.

He stood tall to give directions, and all eyes were on him. There was still shooting going on. It was clear they needed leadership and inspiration, and he was the man that needed to do this. He'd been in these situations before, although never with civilians, and never with his family. While he sometimes wished he was the man following someone else's lead, deep down Vince knew that wasn't his lot in life.

As he spoke to encourage them, the shots grew thicker and he was forced to duck. Some of his words were drowned out in the noise of the engines and gunfire. The group sensed this was their last battle. Their mood shifting to one of grim acceptance and determination, they grabbed their weapons and settled in for their last fight. The women snatched up handguns as if they knew what awaited them if captured. The wounded limped into firing positions. For all his plans, this was all they had left. Desperation wasn't a plan, but it was sure dangerous for the attackers. Vince was so proud of them, his heart was thudding against his chest. His face was wet and not only from the spray of river water. Some came from his eyes as he shed tears of pride for these comrades in arms.

He turned to fight and make the bastards pay dearly.

It was at that moment Vince heard a huge boom roll across the river like a cannon shot. He and his companions ducked.

"What the hell?" Malcolm exclaimed.

Vince knew that sound and couldn't tell at first if hearing it was a reason for joy or terror. It was then that he saw a hole the size of a grapefruit impact one of the boats closing in behind them. The hole was close to the waterline, and in seconds the boat was taking on water much faster than the bilge pumps could bail. That huge boom and the hole in the chasing boat left him both surprised and hopeful.

Vince turned to Malcolm with a huge grin on his face like a Cheshire cat. "That, my friend, is the sound of a fifty caliber. If I was guessing, I'd say it's a Barrett on the ridge with a high-end scope and a skilled sniper behind it. Anyone that man wants dead needs to get gone from this area of the river and fast!"

"What can we do? Do you think he will shoot at us next?" Malcolm asked, his voice high and fast.

Vince put his arm around Malcolm and hugged him close like a brother. "No way, man, that's the cavalry! Our community is on that ridge. The first shot hit their boat, not ours. We made it under the umbrella of artillery coverage! I think it's now safe to say we're gonna be okay!"

The others on the boat heard Vince, and the cheers and jubilation were louder than the shooting had been a few moments earlier. There were hugs and back slaps and grins so wide their faces hurt.

Vince even got a kiss on the lips from a movie star. Before he could ponder whether it meant something or was just exuberance, Liz went to Bert and kissed him on the forehead. Then she hugged Malcolm and kissed him on the cheek. Vince was enjoying the thought that she kissed him on the mouth when she peeked over Malcolm's shoulder and winked. The kiss had been chaste, but the eye contact lingered for a moment longer than needed and left unanswered questions.

Bert began hitting the boat horn in celebration. Ellie went to Malcolm and gave him a big hug and a kiss too. For the first time, Vince didn't feel jealousy or resentment at their happiness, merely a sense of loss. He was happy for them and their shared joy of living through this terrible event. Kate came up from the cabin with a huge grin and hug for her dad, and that meant more than everything else combined.

While Vince couldn't be sure who was behind that big gun, he knew someone who loved shooting those big Barretts. Levi was a master with them. It was too much to hope that it would be him up there, but that man would always have Vince's back when he could. It would be like Uncle Dave to send help if he thought Vince and the town needed the back up.

They heard more big booms, and Vince peered downriver to see the first speed boat powerless and riding lower by the moment in the water, bow first. Then the Barrett shifted to the second boat.

The smaller boats completely forgot about the Sea Ray. They hadn't completely given up the fight, though. In a futile gesture, they were trying to fire uphill at the big Barrett ensconced behind a wall that was almost a mile away. While their weapons might actually carry that far, to think they could aim or hit anything at that range from a boat was ridiculous. As long as the people of the town stayed behind the wall and presented a small target, they were in no danger. Vince even wondered if a shot at that distance from an AR weapon firing a .556 round would still have enough penetration power to kill.

The Sea Ray continued to chug upriver to a dock up ahead and around the bend at the junction of the rivers. It was a little way downriver from the actual city of Carrollton where the charter town sat gleaming on the hill.

The Sea Ray was out of effective range and out of the immediate thoughts of the pursuing boats. It was clear the second pursuit boat was receiving the worst of this gunfire exchange with the big gun on the ridge. The attackers lost interest in Vince's boat and were picking up swimmers from the first boat and soon would be from the second as well.

The gangsters continued to futilely return fire. Those bursts of fire back at the ridge were becoming more sporadic by the minute. The ARs and AKs didn't have the range of the Barrett, and the men weren't exactly sure where to shoot. All they knew was that the big shots were coming from somewhere behind the walls on the ridge.

In the end, two boats were sinking and the third boat was way overloaded with thugs and limping its way back downriver to Madison.

For a moment, the ruthless side of Vince contemplated getting a couple of boats from the community and organizing a chase. The thugs would be sitting ducks. As a military man, Vince knew the community would be safer with those men dead. As an "old" military man and a father, he was bone tired. Tired of fighting and tired of killing.

He wanted to go home and have a beer, a steak, and a nap, in that order.

Those men would have to be dealt with another time. Hopefully they would learn their lesson or be killed by other bad men before they once again became Vince's problem.

Part Thirty-One

HOMECOMING

"New beginnings are often disguised as painful endings."

- Lao Tzu

LIZ

After the echo of the fifty-caliber rifle faded away from the river valley, it was strangely quiet.

Two of the pursuing boats were very low in the water and either smoking or sinking. A third boat was fishing men out of the water and sitting low in the water due to all the extra weight. Whoever was on the hill with the large gun finally took mercy on those men. They were sitting ducks with no way to return fire that far and had quit trying.

As Bert's boat got closer to the mouth of the Little Kentucky River, Vince moved up to stand beside Bert. He directed him to the new dock a little ways inside the mouth of the river on the west bank. Liz followed his glance back at the remaining boat that had pursued them as it limped back downriver. It was nearly lost from sight by this time as it crept east on the Ohio River and Bert's boat passed the point of land going into the Little Kentucky River.

Liz thought she knew Vince fairly well by this time. She believed he was silently hoping it wasn't a mistake to let them go. As mean and ruthless as he could be, she thought Vince Cavanaugh was a good man at heart. He wasn't ready to be so cruel right now as to kill them while they floated helplessly on the water. It was obvious that whoever was behind that big gun apparently agreed.

She couldn't know that Vince was indeed thinking exactly that. Then he moved on to wonder how long it would be before they couldn't afford the luxury of letting bad men live when they had the chance to put them down.

Bert expertly guided the Sea Ray to the dock, about two hundred yards inside the smaller river that emptied into the mighty Ohio. The dock was brand new with three fingers of slips to hold twelve boats. The dock was anchored to a series of large metal poles similar to telephone poles in such a way as to allow the entire dock to float up and down with the water levels. It had power and water connected to the community on the hill.

One of Bert's engines had seized up earlier, and the other engine was smoking by the time they docked. The Sea Ray had taken a tremendous amount of damage.

There was a crowd of people at the dock as Bert gently slid the boat sideways into the dock. Several people rushed forward to take the lines and secure it. They were safe, and their arrival had the feel of a celebrated homecoming. The mood was boisterous, joyous, and even tearful. As a group, a whole lot of tension and fear had finally been released. It was time to celebrate life. The world took a misstep and they survived. With some planning, hard work, and a little luck, they would be the ones that thrived as well.

As they went through the crowd, Vince directed some folks to offload their gear. Their group was given the option to walk up to the charter town on foot or get a ride in a four wheeler or golf cart. Most chose to walk. The whole thing was more like a victory parade than a walk.

Liz was thrilled and surprised beyond words when her grandmother came through the crowd and gave her a huge hug. Dave, in his usual thoughtful attention to detail, made sure some of Liz's family was there to greet her. Liz cried tears of joy and relief and couldn't stop. She hadn't realized how lonely and scared she'd been until she was safe and in her grandmother's arms. She couldn't have explained the range of emotions running through her mind if she'd been asked. Her grandmother sensed it and just squeezed Liz more tightly and patted her back.

When Liz wiped her eyes, she saw that Vince was watching the reunion between her and her grandmother with a smile. At that moment, a huge man wrapped Vince up from behind in a bear hug. Liz didn't know who it was at first. After hearing them talk, she was sure it was Levi, Vince's old buddy.

"Levi! I thought you were in Colorado with my uncle!"

"I was, then he and I thought I'd be more use here."

"Wasn't all air travel grounded as a part of the nationwide declaration of martial law?" Vince asked.

Levi grinned like a Cheshire cat. "Well, you know your uncle. He got some senator to call another and so on until he got our flight designated as critical and providing relief aid. We did have to donate some critical supplies to the police and FEMA workers in Louisville, so here I am, big and beautiful as ever!"

"Did you fly into Louisville?"

"Heck no," Levi said, sounding curiously like Vince's friend Greg. "We went into Springfield, Kentucky. I offloaded the supplies there, and we sent a message to Louisville for their police and FEMA folks to come get their cargo."

Shaking his head, he said, "I'm surprised they went for that."

"They didn't have much choice. We mentioned shots fired and damage and garble this and that. They're government and are used to fubar things. Besides, what can they do about it? It's free stuff, if they want to send a team down to Springfield."

"I had no idea you were coming. We did get a couple of calls through. I would have thought Uncle Dave would have told us. Not that I'm complaining, mind you!"

"We didn't know ourselves that I was coming until late in your operation. By that time, there was only one more call that got through. Besides, we didn't think there was any way the knowledge would have helped you in the field. We still aren't sure who is monitoring those SAT phone signals. So we decided only to use them in a way that sounded like family members checking in on each other."

"I get it, and you're probably right. I can tell you, I've never been more happy in my life than when I heard that big Barrett booming down from the ridge!"

"That's not true," Levi said.

"What do you mean?" Vince asked, confused.

"You seemed pretty happy when I gave you a big hug!" Levi pinched Vince's cheek, then pulled him into a bear hug and whispered in his ear, "Or perhaps the most happy moment has something do with why that movie star keeps watching you so intently."

Malcolm and Ellie were holding hands as they walked up the hill. This was all brand new, and he was out of his element. Ellie was familiar with the area and several of the people. Only the walled town at the top of the hill was new to her. What was important was that they had the whole family together and they were safe.

Even Kate, who was bummed at the prospect of leaving Chicago and moving back to the "sticks," was in a buoyant mood. A lot of her happiness was probably due to her escape from death or worse at the hands of the thugs who chased them down the river. Yet it was hard for her to hide a huge smile when she saw a tall, good-looking young man who helped her off the boat and onto the dock.

"Matt? Oh my God, is that you? You're so different!"

Matt blushed and replied shyly, "I've been working out and lost some weight."

Liz noticed that both Vince and Ellie witnessed the exchange as well. Ellie's smile indicated that she liked the tall, good-looking young man as well.

Vince's face displayed his confusion. Since a lot of dads lost track of their kids' friends, that didn't surprise Liz. It must have been harder for Vince, because Kate had been living in Chicago. After a moment, Vince's face changed as he placed Matt. Judging by Kate's response to Matt, he had changed more than "just working out some."

"You're a lot taller too," Kate said to Matt.

Her voice sounded more reserved and shy to Liz than it had been the entire trip. Kate was beaming. She would have been embarrassed to know how obvious she was to the others around her.

Good for her, Liz thought. She needed a friend like Matt. The interest of a tall, good-looking young man was the perfect medicine for Kate.

The entire group began walking up the hill in a slow, joyous procession. The walled city on a hill held a commanding view of both rivers and the surrounding valley. Some of their gear was being taken off the boat and carted up the hill.

For Liz and most of the crowd, it felt good to stretch their legs and let some of the stress drain away. It was only a few moments ago she thought for sure they would be killed or captured.

Vince and Levi were walking beside Bert as they went up the hill.

"I promise to get your boat fixed, Bert. You saved our lives. It may take a few days to find the parts the way things are now, though."

"Thanks, Vince. I do love that old boat. I trust you. I like what you folks are doing here too."

"We'd like to have you stay a few days if you want. I'd love to show you around to see what we're doing here," Vince said enthusiastically.

"I appreciate that," Bert said, "but I have family and friends in Hanover who are worried about me. We have a pretty secure spot back there too as long as we all work together. They need me, and I don't want to worry them any more than I have."

"I totally get it. Levi and I can take you downriver by some back roads I know to a spot across the river from your home this evening. From there, we can get you across the river via an inflatable. We'll leave as soon as it's dark if that works for you."

"Works for me. Although I think we need to avoid Milton on the Kentucky side of Madison. I'm not sure how much of that chaos has spread to Milton and how much of it the Madison gang controls."

"You're right, we'll stay on the ridge and a few miles south of Milton. Is tonight soon enough for you? I'd leave sooner, but I don't want the bad guys to see us leaving in case they're watching. I also don't want to draw attention to your group by crossing the river in daylight."

"Yep, that will work. Plus, it gives me a few hours to see what you all have built here."

———

As dusk was covering the ridge and river valley, Liz stood on the walls gazing down the river. Vince, Levi, and Bert had left a little while ago to get Bert back to his home and family. Even though it was nicer and safer here, Bert was drawn to his own home and people. He didn't feel yet that things were so bad he needed to come here to keep his family safe. They assured him he was welcome if and when that time came.

Liz knew the Colorado charter town was the home she had planned for. It was much larger and better appointed than this location. Colorado had everything anyone could want in terms of beauty, luxury, and supplies to keep them fed and safe not only for years, but decades if needed.

This place and these people felt more like home. It was comforting to see faces she'd known before she was famous and who spoke like her. She was confident they had her best interests at heart. She needed the downtime and some family to hold close during the hard times.

After all, weren't home and hearth what it was all about?

AFTERWORD

I want to thank each one of you reading this, for your time and interest in this story.

My hope is that we can find common ground on a vision of what *could* be and you'll feel entertained and see it in your mind as I do.

As with many people who write, I have dozens of stories in my head fighting to get out and be put on paper.

Quite frankly, I gravitate to Dystopian and Post-Apocalyptic stories because I feel they are timely, and like most of you I walk through life with the constant hum of *"what if"* deep in my brain. Most importantly though, I choose to write in this genre for you all! I like that people enjoy these stories and can share my vision. I like the interaction on social media and when we meet at public events.

Please feel free to reach out to me on Facebook at *Author D.A. Carey* or on my website, WWW.DACarey.com. There is a blue sign-up button on my webpage for my newsletter that I send out sparingly. It will have information about upcoming books, events, and giveaways that I hope you'll enjoy. I can be e-mailed at DACarey@DACarey.com.

Again, thank *you*... As people who read and enjoy these stories there can be no higher compliment than the time you spend taking this journey with me.

ACKNOWLEDGMENTS

For my family, friends, and workmates, I thank you so much for the times you have sat around a campfire, dinner table, or the workplace and listened to me spin a yarn. Your patience and positive support is why this story came into being.

Special thanks to Felicia A. Sullivan, who gave me encouragement and direction when I really needed it. She is the difference between a great story in my mind and one on paper. Her support and advice went well past the scope of what I could have expected.

Finally, many other authors in this genre have been so gracious and nice that I want to thank them. My only concern is that I'll miss someone. Steven C. Bird and Chris Pike were both kind enough to offer feedback and support early on that meant more to me than they know. L.L. Akers is a great author and has graciously given of her time and knowledge, just as Boyd Craven and Jeff Motes have. Franklin Horton is great guy, as are Doug Hogan and A. American.

I also can't forget to mention Annie Berdel and Dee Cooper as well, who have both gone above and beyond to help and advise.

These are some truly great authors and I encourage to you check out their books if you haven't already. You'll enjoy many nights curled up in the world they'll create in your minds.

WWW.DACAREY.COM

Thank You for Reading Arks of America.

If you enjoyed this novel, I'd be very appreciative if you'd take a moment to write a short review and post it on Amazon. A few words is all it takes.

Amazon uses a complex formula to determine what books are recommended to readers or show up in the search functions. How many books sell are only one small part of the formula. The quantity of reviews are also an important factor.

Also, don't forget to sign up!...I choose to write in this genre for you all! I like that people enjoy these stories and who can share my vision. I like the interaction on social media and when we meet at public events. Please feel free to reach out to me on Facebook at Author D. A. Carey or on my website, WWW.DACarey.com. There is a blue sign-up button on my webpage for my newsletter that I send out sparingly. It will have information about upcoming books, events and giveaways that I hope you'll enjoy. I can be e-mailed at DACarey@DACarey.com.

ABOUT THE AUTHOR

D. A. Carey is an army veteran that comes from a line of Army veterans on both sides. After moving around a lot and finally settling in North Central Kentucky as a kid, he grew up with a step-family of Kentucky do-it-yourself country people who made the discussion of history and "Foxfire" skills a regular part of dinner conversation, giving a perspective that not everyone has. He enjoys sharing private family stories with his readers and followers.

Charit Creek, as titled in Book 2, is a *real* place, and while Carey has a day-job in the white-collar world of technology leadership, he still manages to make time to hunt, ride horses, hike, and camp—and continues to commit time to one of the highlights of his year in an annual trip to Big South Fork – Charit Creek, in the more wild woods of Tennessee. During this trip, 10-15 men ride out on horseback for several days, carrying only what they can fit in their saddle bags, to immerse themselves in nature. Feel free to follow him on social media for a closer look at his yearly adventure, and the real "Charit Creek."

f

BOOKS BY D.A. CAREY

The Arks Chronicles

Book 1: *Arks of America*

Book 2: *Charit Creek*

Book 3: *Eastern Chaos: Ten Kingdoms*

Book 4: *The Badlands: Ten Kingdoms...coming soon*

Arks of America
by D.A. Carey
Copyright © D.A. Carey 2018. All Rights Reserved.

- Cover art by Deranged Doctor Designs
- Editing by Felicia Sullivan
- Proofreading by Jessica Meigs
- Formatting by L.L. Akers

Made in the USA
Columbia, SC
14 February 2024